I'm Makin' It My Business

To dear friends Ginny & David,
Thanks for your support & discussion
About the book. I Am Thankful
for friends like you.
—Neill Little

Neill Little

Also by Neill Little

A Badge in His Pocket and a Banjo on His Knee

This book is a work of fiction. All characters in the novel are fictitious. Any resemblance to actual events or locales or persons, living or dead is entirely coincidental.

ISBN-13: 978057886813

Printed by

Kindle Direct Publishing, an Amazon.com Company

Available from Amazon.com and other online stores

Available on Kindle and other devices

Printed in the United States of America

Cover Photograph by Rebecca Little

1st Edition May 2021

Acknowledgements

to

My incredible family, who make life interesting and fun, and encouraged me to take another stab at writing.

The many friends who enjoyed my first book and also encouraged me to write again.

The Three Amigas - Kimberly England, Phyllis Alexander, and Vickie Turbeville who gave me a blank journal for writing notes that led to this book.

Kindle Direct Publishing for their publishing expertise.

Mystery Writers of America - New England Chapter and their wonderful staff of instructors.

Bo Turner, Chad Pace, and Eric Jouberts for their technical expertise.

Mike Coleman, Marc Overlock, Nancy Bass, and Laura Dannemiller who proofread the book and suggested edits.

Christy Lejeune, my tireless editor who found time during a pandemic, raising two children and writing in her own job, to review my work many times. Thank you for helping me bring these words to life and making edits that enriched the story.

Rebecca, my wife, for supporting me in this project and allowing me time to sit quietly somewhere and craft a story, for reviewing this book in her own way, for giving constructive criticism, and for encouraging me to write this second book.

Chapter One

*I*t was around noon one hot August day. I was enjoying an iced coffee and reading *The Tennessean* newspaper online when I heard a car door slam shut down in the parking lot outside my office window followed by the sound of someone running through the gravel and onto the wood deck behind the building. I scooted my chair toward the window and spotted a metallic blue Maserati Ghibli, which I recognized by the distinctive trident on the grill. The driver parked in such a way that nobody else could get out of our parking area till they moved the car. I never cared for presumptuous people who pulled stunts like that.

The sound of heavy shoes resounding on the center stairwell startled me, but not as much as the casually dressed man carrying a package who suddenly appeared at my office door and quickly let himself inside.

"Hey!! I'm in a hurry!" he said frantically, out of breath and sweating. "Open this and read the directions inside! And check out my car! It's important!"

I looked out the window, took note of the car again and heard the wail of sirens nearby, but my office was close to a fire hall and police station, so that wasn't unusual. The sirens got his attention, though, as the mysterious stranger jerked to glance out the window, too.

Then he leaned over, pointed a finger at me and said with a scowl, "Don't come looking for me, man, 'cause you'll never find me! I'm invisible, someone nobody knows, just doing my job. Now you do yours!"

He shoved the package across the desk so hard that it slammed onto my chest, and then he ran out the door.

"Hey, buddy! Come back here! What's this all about?" I yelled after him.

My words were in vain; he was already down the stairs and halfway to the car. I looked out the window to check the license number, but he backed out of the lot and into the alley in such a way that I couldn't see it. The sirens died and the blue car sped north, out of sight.

The name's Max; Max Jackson. I've been a PI in South Nashville for the past ten years. I work on the third floor out of this mansion of sorts, a rambling old place just off 21st Avenue that was refurbished into offices for chumps like me who can't afford anything more elegant and don't want to be in the high-rent district, anyway. The majestic house is three stories high and made of stone, with ivy growing up its sides in places, but neatly trimmed around the windows. High tin ceilings make for cool and drafty winters and hot and stuffy summers on the upper floors on a day like today. Old wood floors and an impressive center staircase give the place a world of charm. That's more than I can say for the building's occupants.

Working here are a couple of psychologists, a divorce lawyer, programmers with a small software company, a freelance writer and me—all people who want a quiet space in which to get our work done. We stay out of each others' hair and everybody gets along. On the first floor, there's a hip coffee shop, The Happy Bean and Bagel, that caters mainly to students in the area and folks living nearby. When they're open, the entire building has the luscious smell of freshly baked cinnamon bread and hazelnut coffee.

My home is the "New Nashville," the one where not only musicians but also young people with all sorts of talent move to seek fame and fortune. It's different from the Bible Belt city that used to grow quietly, back when I was a kid, in the shadow of the capital of the South—Atlanta—and was now a cool place to live, work and party. Nashville had been the "Athens of the South," so called because of the Parthenon replica in the middle of Centennial Park; "Music City U.S.A.," because of the recording industry; and was now the "Bachelorette Party City of the U.S." My, how times have changed. Still, it's a great place to live and is home for me. Always has been.

To have some guy storm up the stairs, crash into my office and leave about as noisily as he entered, well, that didn't do anything for my standing in the office building, whatever that was. After he left, one of the shrinks came out into the hall, looked through my full-glass office door and asked in a "I'm just checking on you and don't really want to get involved" sort of way if everything was okay. I nodded yes and apologized.

Michelle, the writer down the hall, opened my office door and asked what was going on. She always did seem more personable than the rest, even though I didn't know her that well.

"I'm fine. Sorry about the racket, Michelle. Usually, my clients call or have an appointment. That guy just stormed in, left me a package and took off." I don't know why I told her about the package. It just sort of came out.

"Ooooh! That's mysterious. What's in it?" she asked and looked inquisitively at the box wrapped in plain brown paper, tied with a green jute string and addressed to me in an almost illegible Sharpie scrawl. "It's got your name on it," she said.

"How about that? Listen, Michelle, I don't want you getting involved in anything you'd regret later. Maybe you ought to get back to work."

"Oh, I'm not really busy. I'm working on a piece about a supposedly haunted house, and frankly, it's getting a little creepy. I could use a distraction. Besides, we've worked next door to each other for a year and I really haven't gotten to meet you. I'm Michelle McCartney, as in Paul, except I play guitar right-handed. Being the investigative type, you probably figured that out about me already."

Michelle was quite pretty, and unusually pleasant company to keep in this dreary PI business. Even though I was itching to see what was in the package, I didn't want to run her off. The benefit of her staying was that if I got killed opening the package, she could tell the cops what happened.

"Nice to officially meet you, Michelle," I said. "I've seen your name on the sign at your door and downstairs in the directory. The calluses on your hand tell me you really are a guitar player —but who isn't in this town? We've got more musicians than lawyers here, and that's sayin' something. I also know that you don't park your car in a garage at home because it's never clean, and you've got bird crap on the roof most of the time. You must run or exercise regularly since there's a gym bag in the passenger seat of your car." *And you have a nice butt*—but I didn't say that. "Friday is probably your night on the town since you always wear a skirt and blouse instead of the usual pants and sweater on other days, like today. And you like Asian food for lunch because that's what the hallway smells like after you bring it back to the office around twelve thirty. I don't see how you can eat that stuff every single day!"

"My, someone has been paying attention. And to clarify my eating habits, I have vegetarian on Wednesdays," she said, hands on her hips. "As long as we're playing the Sherlock Holmes game, I'd say you're single—no ring. Plus, you keep odd hours, and I've noticed that your shirt and tie don't often match. You don't ever seem to get the blues right. And why do you bother wearing a tie these days? Most of the time you look like you don't sleep well and you forget to finish brushing your hair. The part in the back is messy, like today. A loving wife wouldn't let you out of the house looking like that. You eat lunch on the desk and are sort of sloppy, leaving sandwich wrappers around. I'd hate to think what your home or apartment looks like."

"Your attempts at charming me aren't working, sweetheart. How about the pistol under my jacket or the slight limp in my left leg."

"I know about the pistol and I didn't want to mention the limp," she said. "I thought that would be rude. I also think you're a lonely man."

"The limp's from a car accident, but that's another story. And lonely kind of goes with the job."

We looked at each other for a moment, evidently content with personal analysis, round one. We both smiled.

"All right, let's see what's in this package," I said.

I reached in my pocket and pulled out my dad's old Barlow knife. The string on the package snapped when it hit the razor-sharp edge, and the paper wrapped around the box fell open slightly. I gently pulled it back, half expecting it to blow up or have something deadly inside. But it was just a shoe box— New Balance NB1's, to be exact. I slowly pulled back the top and found tissue paper covering the contents.

"What's inside?" Michelle asked excitedly.

"I don't know. I haven't gotten to the good part yet," I said. "And what are you hangin' around here for? This is a private matter. Isn't it time for you to run out for sushi or something?"

She backed away from the desk and said, "I guess so, but I'm still curious about the box."

"Yeah, well, you know what that did for the cat. If I find anything you can help me with, you'll be the first to know. Now, scram before I quit being so nice to you."

Michelle chuckled and sashayed out the door and down the hall, distracting me as much leaving the room as she had while she was in it.

But back to the matter at hand. I pulled back the tissue paper and discovered a printed page of paper, some five-by-seven photographs, a jump drive, and a business envelope addressed to me with the return address of a law firm in Atlanta. The envelope figured to be the best place to start, so I retrieved the knife and carefully slit it open.

Inside was a letter and two Madisons—two $5,000 dollar bills! The letter read:

Mr. Jackson,

Please accept the enclosed cash for your services. If the job described below is completed within thirty days, another 10K will be delivered to you. Our client wishes to remain anonymous and wants to keep this matter from local authorities. You and anyone you employ in this investigation must agree to these terms.

You were selected because of your familiarity with the area and the obscurity of your firm.

Please insert the alpha-numeric jump drive in your computer for further information.

This was getting interesting! And how about that—the obscurity of my firm. That sounds like a nice way to say nobody's heard of me before. Still, that kind of money sure was nice. Though I've learned that sometimes, big money accompanies big risks.

Chapter Two

I plugged in the long jump drive, which had a very small keyboard on the top. After it loaded for several seconds, a message popped up on my screen.

Text "Ready" to the burner cell phone number listed below. You will receive an encrypted email one minute after you send the text. There will be only four numbers in the email. One minute after the email is sent, you will receive a text with four numbers from this phone number. Enter the make of the car (lowercase) used to deliver this package and then the email number followed by the text number you receive (no spaces between each) on the jump drive keyboard. A file will unlock. Read it carefully and make notes. The file is protected so it cannot be printed. The password on the jump drive will be randomized after being open for five minutes, and you will not be able to reopen the file. At that time, data on the jump drive will also be scrambled to an unreadable form.

As directed, I texted "Ready" to the cell phone number shown. Shortly afterwards I received an email from NOREPLY with the numbers 2957. And then a return text arrived with the numbers 7865. Now all I had to do was to enter maserati followed by the two sequences of numbers. The keyboard on the jump drive was tiny, so much so that I had to use the end of a paperclip to enter the password, maserati29577865. When I touched the last number 5, the file opened.

The Word file described a woman who lived in Nashville with a rich uncle in Atlanta. He was a widow, had no kids, worked all the time, got rich in real estate, and was considering willing everything to her before he died and distant relatives staked a claim. He was dying of some incurable disease and they wanted me to check out the niece to make sure she was worthy of receiving his fortune—he *thought* she was, but what did he know.

It was an interesting story, but I shook my head in disgust, tired of all the smoke-and-dagger mystery. I clicked on Google and looked online for the phone number of the Kubrick, Goldmeister and Klein law firm in Atlanta. I found it and made a call.

A very proper-speaking, non-Southern sounding receptionist answered. I asked to speak to Mr. Kubrick, figuring since he got top billing in the firm name, he would be the head honcho and would know about this package.

"I'm sorry, but Mr. Kubrick is not available," the woman on the other end answered. "May I ask who is calling and the nature of your business?" she asked.

"Sure you can ask. My name's Max Jackson, from Nashville. I just received a package delivered by a crazy man on behalf of your firm. It had pictures, a jump drive and ten thousand dollars in cash inside to pique my interest. The jump drive had some information about a wealthy old man who wants to check up on a niece to see if she's worthy of an inheritance. You can tell Mr. Kubrick if he wants me to do this job, he's going to have to call me or come up here and talk face-to-face. Sending strange packages almost anonymously is no way to do business! Especially with me! I bet Kubrick's got a cell phone. Have him call me this afternoon before I leave at five or I'm shipping this stuff pronto back to your office complete with the cash. Any questions?"

"Why, why no, Mr. Jackson. I will express your concerns to Mr. Kubrick immediately. Is there anything else I should tell Mr. Kubrick?"

"Yeah. While you're at it, tell him nobody in their right mind delivers packages driving a Maserati! Around here anyway. They kind of stand out. Especially the metallic blue ones."

"Yes sir. The blue ones. I'll pass that along. Good afternoon, Mr. Jackson."

"Thanks," I replied and hung up the phone, right about the time there was a knock on the door. It was Michelle – and she was already opening it and stepping inside.

"Sorry to disturb you Max, but I couldn't help but hear some of your conversation," she said.

"When you've got your ear hangin' out an open door eavesdropping, things like that happen, Michelle. Come on in," I said as I made a sweeping motion with my hand. "Sorry I was loud, it's just that it rubs me the wrong way when people get too fancy with technology just to look smart. I've learned that when cases start like that, the ground rules for communicating are established and they rarely work. It takes forever to get things done and the other guys always seem to be calling the shots. Think about it. If these lawyers were trying to be so secretive, why did they send me cash with the return address of their law firm on the package? Somebody's not thinkin' straight down there."

Michelle looked at the items on the desk and asked, "Do you mind if I look at these pictures?"

"No, go ahead. I'm fixin' to pack all this stuff up and return it to the geniuses in Atlanta, anyway."

"Hmm," she said, studying one of the photos. "I know this girl from somewhere. Let me think. Oh yeah, her name's Cassie! She's done some fill-in teaching at the CoreStrength gym I go to. Talk about a woman with abs of steel!"

I studied the first few photos, which appeared to be candid shots of this Cassie woman in an exercise class of some kind. Another captured her in downtown Franklin looking in the window at one of those stores on Main Street with beautiful clothes, high rent, and few shoppers. Another showed her putting a few bucks in the case of a guy playing guitar on a street corner by the coffee shop. The last was of her getting out of her car, a late model beige Subaru Crosstrek, complete with a bike rack on the roof and a Radnor Lake vanity license plate. She was wearing the same clothes and the sky was sunny as in the last three pictures, so I assumed they were all taken on the same day.

"Why would someone drop off pictures of Cassie to you? Is she in some kind of trouble?" Michelle asked.

"Not really. The raised voice you heard was me telling the folks in Atlanta what I thought about their package. Whatever's going on is no concern of mine now. I've got to get back to work on the case of 'Can you find the extremely valuable guitar my crazy wife sold at a pawn shop when she got mad just because I bought another extremely valuable guitar?' The guy's a lead twanger in a well-known band, and his wife doesn't like his ever-growing collection of instruments, the time he spends on the road with the band, or, if I'd had my guess, the way he ogles the lead singer in the short skirt when I've seen them play, but that's his problem."

"Still, I wonder about Cassie," Michelle said. "She seems to be pretty normal, not that I know her all that well. Even though our regular instructor is good, everyone likes it when she teaches, too. We nicknamed her the 'Planking Queen' since she makes us hold planks for two minutes at least, but it seems like an hour."

She paused and examined one of the photos again.

"There must be a good reason someone sent you these photos, Max. Maybe you oughta check it out."

"Don't wanna know. Don't care. Here. Put the photos in the box so I can return this stuff."

About then, my phone, which was sitting on the desk, rang. The caller ID showed an Area Code of 678. Michelle and I looked at each other. "That's an Atlanta number. Are you going to answer?" she asked.

I nodded at her and picked up the phone. "Jackson," I answered.

"Mr. Jackson," said the caller in his slow, deep, Southern drawl, obviously using a speakerphone. "This is Josef Kubrick from Atlanta. Might I have a few moments of your extremely valuable time?"

Chapter Three

"**M**r. Kubrick," I said, surprised. I hadn't expected him to return my call. "What's a hotshot big-city lawyer from Atlanta want with a two-bit gumshoe like me? I was just repacking the box I received from you today and gettin' ready to return it to the sender. That would have to be you or someone in your office."

The voice on the other end laughed and said, "Hold on before you finish packing. I didn't expect your negative response to our generous offer, Mr. Jackson. Most PIs wouldn't turn down ten thousand dollars with the promise of more on the way for a simple job like this. What do ya say about giving me a second chance? I need this done for a very important longtime friend and client, and I want to do all I can for him."

"I imagine the payday for your firm is pretty sweet, too, isn't it Mr. Kubrick? You've probably already got a good bit invested so far and don't have anything to show, so your client is getting antsy and thinking about finding a new lawyer. Out of curiosity, what makes you think I'm the man for the job?" I asked.

"Well, to be honest, you're about the right age and have some experience, you're not in a big firm so we can keep this matter private, and you seem to have the toughness that it might take to get the facts we need. If you want the job, the money's yours. What da ya say?" he asked.

"You've piqued my interest. But before we sign anything, tell me what's going on. The file said something about a man who's dying and wants to bequeath his fortune to a relative who lives here. You want me to make sure she's not an ax murderer or something like it. Is that about right? I still don't see what the big deal is," I said.

"Well, there are a few minor details we need to discuss," he offered.

"What kind of *minor* details?" I asked. "Are they the kind that'll make me wish I never took this case in the first place?"

"I doubt it, Mr. Jackson. So, are you game?" He asked the question in such a way that I could tell this was his final offer before he pulled it and looked for somebody else.

"Well, I could use a little excitement around here. Besides, I haven't been on a stakeout in six months. Count me in. And call me Max—that Mr. Jackson stuff is way more respectful than I usually get or deserve, and makes me want an antacid. Now, about those details …"

"Very well, Max. Let's start from the beginning. My client started a garden supply company many years ago and became quite successful. His company added locations in several parts of Atlanta, all of which were adjacent to new suburbs. The city kept growing, and his properties became extremely valuable for development purposes, so he eventually sold out. During his working years, he was a disciplined investor in Atlanta companies and put every extra dollar he could into Coca-Cola, Home Depot, SunTrust and UPS stocks. Needless to say, his small fortune grew into a large one. He and his wife never had children; no bundles of joy meant big bundles of cash left for them. They lived modestly, but gave freely, supporting a musician's chair in the symphony— a bassoonist, oddly enough —which meant he paid the guy's salary every year. Another favorite charity has been the botanical gardens, as you might expect—being gardeners and all—as well as their church. There's a stained-glass window in a downtown Episcopal church on Peachtree with their names engraved on a gold plate, right next to St. Peter's left foot. I see it every Sunday."

"Okay, so the guy's got a lot of dough. Doesn't his wife get it when he dies?" I asked.

"Under Georgia law, she would, but she passed away recently from a ruptured aneurysm. No one saw it coming. She was trimming their prize roses in the backyard garden and keeled over right into one of the bushes. Shortly after the funeral, my client went for a checkup with his doctor—he was concerned that the same thing might happen to him, as if that sort of thing was catching. He was pretty healthy, but had recently experienced some migraine-like headaches. They cleared him of aneurysm concerns, but found a marble-sized tumor at the base of his brain that was evidently the cause of the headaches. It's wrapped around the spinal cord and surgery would be too dangerous. They give him three months, tops. That's why the rush to get this deal done."

"Sounds like the guy can't buy a break lately," I said. "So he's concerned about what's going to happen to his dough when he kicks the bucket. Is there anyone who he doesn't want to get the money?"

"Any one of questionable character, he tells me. He doesn't have any siblings, but his wife has three, and they've got kids, and that's where it gets messy. There's a niece, Cassie Simpshire, the focus of our attention; a nephew, Sammy Simpshire, a step-nephew, Gabriel Farasinni; and a step-niece, Eulala (Layla) Farasinni. That's about all the folks that count as family. Each one gets a few grand every year from my client and may be expecting a big payout when he passes. Mind you, only the doc and my client, and now the two of us, know about the tumor. The niece Cassie is the one he thinks he wants the money to go to because she's always been the favorite of him and his wife. When Cassie was a little girl, she used to spend summers with them in Atlanta and would help in the garden. My client was also a hobbyist rose breeder and developed a beautiful, bright red variety that he only sold in his garden stores. He named it for her—*The Cassie*. He thought it was providential that his wife collapsed into the Cassie rose bush when she died. You know, sort of a sign from heaven that Cassie should inherit his fortune."

I thought for a moment and wondered how many people really did have this sort of a problem. I was fortunate enough to have a nephew and three nieces, and they all seemed like good kids. Of course, the youngest was two and the oldest was eight years old, so they hadn't really had time to get in major trouble. If I had an inheritance to share, it would go to all four of them in equal shares.

"Sounds like it," I said. "Why doesn't he just give the inheritance to her, leave the others out of it, and call it a day?"

He paused for a moment then said, "That would make it easier. But he wants to be double-sure she's worthy, you know that she's wise with money, a good person, and that sort of thing. Of course, there's his wife's sister and brother as potential inheritance candidates, too, but they're both way up in years and have flat-out said they don't want his money because of some kind of family spat that goes way back. Must have been pretty serious to not want twenty-million dollars! There's one other thing I forgot to mention. Another step-nephew died suddenly a few weeks ago, so he's out of the picture."

"So all you want me to do is follow the gal here in Nashville, make sure she's not a nutcase of some kind, and give you the go-ahead to make her the heir to the old man's fortune? Right? How much time do you have and how much information do you want?" I asked, wondering if this was going to be as easy as it appeared.

"We'd like to wrap it up by the end of the month—no later than three weeks from today. We'll present your findings and do the paperwork for whatever my client desires. Just keep track of the girl's daily habits and let us know if anything looks suspicious. If it doesn't work out for her, and the others are bad eggs like my client suspects, the low double-reeds section in the Atlanta symphony and roses in the botanical gardens are sitting on a nice payday. As executors, we come out the same either way."

"I'm glad to hear that! Heaven forbid the ambulance chasers don't get a piece of the action," I chuckled.

I heard the voice of another person I didn't know was listening in the background cackle at my comment.

"That's pretty good, Jackson!" he responded. "I'm just sorry this is probably the only opportunity we'll have to work together. If there were more, I'm certain I'd find more things to dislike about you. Lord knows the list is growing, but I must say you do find humor in life situations."

"Alright Kubrick, I'll see what I can find out about this Cassie girl. For her sake and mine, too, let's hope she's walkin' the straight and narrow. I've got the photos and personal information right here. What da ya say I give you a call in a week with an initial report? Sooner, if I find out something," I said, hoping this was going to be an easy job that I could wrap up quickly.

I thought of one more thing. "And by the way Mr. Kubrick ... about my payment. Where's a guy supposed to use a couple of five thousand dollar bills anyway? I don't think they give change for those at Taco Bell, even if you get a burrito supreme meal."

He laughed. "I bet they don't. The next ten thousand will be on a nice official check from our firm when we receive your report. I suggest you go to the main branch of your bank and they'll swap those two bills for some that are easier to spend. Dress nicely when you go and don't act suspicious," he suggested.

"Roger that. You'll be hearing from me, Kubrick."

"Good afternoon, Jackson."

The line went dead.

That afternoon I went to my bank's headquarters downtown to deposit the money in my bank account. Having ten thousand dollars in cash in my wallet made me feel like a marked man as I parked my car and walked down the street toward the bank entrance. I usually had only twenty bucks or so on me, if I had that much.

I hoped my casual outfit—a collared polo shirt, khakis, and dress shoes—would make a better statement to the clerk than the t-shirt, shorts, and running shoes I'd normally wear on a day like today.

As I approached the teller's window, the overly friendly clerk said, "Good morning, sir! How may I help you?"

She was probably glad to see me since I was one of only two customers in this huge lobby with ten or more service windows ready to transact business. I figured with online banking being what it was, there wasn't much in-person banking done these days, except for getting a loan which I didn't want. Having another bill to pay was the last thing *I* needed.

"Yes, ma'am. I'm here to make a deposit," I answered. I opened up my wallet, pulled out the two five-thousand dollar bills, and handed them to her with a deposit slip I had filled out at home.

"Oh, my! We don't see these very often. How did you come by them?" she asked curiously.

I figured she was legally required to ask when such big bills came in, so I decided not to give her a hard time about that being none of her business.

"One of my clients decided to pay me in cash instead of a check," I answered. I decided she didn't need to know exactly how they came to me in the package delivered by a madman.

"I wonder if he had a reason for doing that?" she asked without looking up at me.

"I wonder, too. It would have been a lot easier just to write a check, if you ask me."

"So what kind of work gets paid for in $5,000 bills instead of a check that can be traced back to the bank?" she asked as she pushed her reading glasses to the tip of her nose and looked over them at me.

"If you have to know, I'm a private detective, and I'm doing work for a lawyer in Atlanta. I think he sent me the bills to get my attention. He certainly accomplished that and cost me a lot of time getting them deposited, too," I answered, just stating the facts and getting a little irritated with how long this process was taking.

"I see," she said, typing something in her computer. Then her printer produced a stamped deposit slip, which she handed to me.

With the same smile I saw before the interrogation, she handed it to me and said, "Good luck with your detective work, Mr. Jackson. Have a nice day!"

Evidently, I'd passed with the test and was free to leave the building. I walked cautiously out the doors, semi-expecting a couple of Homeland Security agents to grab me once I exited the building, but nothing happened, so I took a deep breath of relief and headed back to the office.

Chapter Four

I studied the photos of Cassie Simpshire and read the printed page included in the package. Cute gal, twenty-eight years old, long, dark brown hair with a little wave, prominent dark eyes, average height and weight, with squared shoulders like a swimmer. Lives alone in a multi-unit apartment just off Music Row near Belmont University. Graduated from Belmont in marketing with a minor in exercise science. Manages a trendy women's athletic apparel shop in the Gulch. Teaches aerobics and yoga occasionally. Distance runner. Likes flowers. Has lived in town five years and travels to Atlanta for two of the three big holidays—July 4th, Thanksgiving or Christmas—and goes there on weekends sporadically.

My plan was to stake out her apartment, check out where she worked and tail her to see if she went anywhere interesting. I sure as hell wasn't going to take an aerobics class or run wherever she did. I'd just have to assume she stayed out of trouble in those places. And I'd check her out online to see what was there. I could also enlist my office neighbor Michelle to get some information, since she already sort of knew Cassie and seemed interested in the case.

The drive to Cassie's apartment this particular afternoon wasn't too challenging since it was just before rush hour (which seems to start earlier every year). Three brave cyclists wearing matching black and yellow shirts with MHB printed on the back were zipping down Wedgewood, keeping pace with my grey Altima SR. There must be hundreds of Altimas in town, probably because Nissan's headquarters was just down the road in Franklin. I like mine because it blends in well with other vehicles and doesn't look suspicious on stakeouts. It also has a killer sound system and enough horsepower to catch up with most anyone I'm following.

Cassie's apartment was in a cool old house that favored my office building, except smaller, with dark red brick instead of my antique white. There wasn't a chimney, either, or a coffee shop downstairs, and hers was a place to live in, instead of work, so maybe they weren't that much alike after all. The black shutters needed painting and there were a few loose clay tiles on the east side second-story roof. Otherwise, it looked pretty good. Landscaping was minimal, and the shrubbery had seen better days, but with Nashville's hot, dry summers, most everything else in town was looking parched, too.

Across the street and one house down to the right was a place being renovated, like so many others in the area. That seemed to be the fate of these 1940s- and '50s-era homes; move the old people out, renovate, then charge an arm and a leg for rent to the next suckers that move in. Out front of this place, a big roll-off container full of discarded wood was parked beside saw horses and a pile of two-by-fours and plywood still wrapped and sealed with a metal band. The gravel drive went up a slight hill and circled left, around the back of the house. This looked like a perfect vantage point for me to watch what was going on at Cassie's place.

I drove up to the house like I was somebody, got out of the car and told one of the workers I wanted to speak to the foreman. The worker was Hispanic and may not have understood everything I said, but he went and got a guy named Manuel who turned out to be the straw boss. I quickly flashed my PI license to the guy and started talking.

"Manuel, the name's Max Jackson. *Buenos dias.*"

"*Buenos dias, Señor,* Jackson. Is anything wrong?"

"No," I said. "I'm working undercover for the construction company doing this and other job sites in the area. It seems that building material is being stolen from rehab jobs and they want me to check some nights and try to catch anyone helping themselves to the supplies. I plan to be here a few nights the next couple of weeks to investigate. I just wanted to let you know."

"Sure, Mr. Jackson. My men are very honest. They never steal," Manuel said in better English than some of my own kin, most of whom were born and raised here.

"I'm not accusing you or your men of anything Manuel. It's some guys that work for another rehab construction company in town that are the problem. Moved here from out-of-state. Our guys think they're trying to run us and others out of business by stealing our stuff. That's why they called me."

I wasn't sure the guy was buying my story, but at least he hadn't given me any grief. He seemed genuinely interested.

"And don't tell your boss, Manuel," I continued. "I'm supposed to do this without you knowing I'm here at night. He just wants to make sure his supplies are safe. I'll be sure to stick up for you and your guys."

"*Gracias*, Señor Jackson," he said. "I must get back to work now. I'll tell my workers that you might be here sometimes."

I studied Cassie's apartment across the street and didn't see anyone around. No cars were parked out front and there weren't any in the driveway, either. I couldn't tell if there were any out back. I got in the car, drew a quick sketch of the house as well as those on either side of it, then got out of the car and walked over.

A large square stone walkway led from the sidewalk to two steps at the front porch, which curved all the way around the right side of the house. The rock steps were worn from many years of people taking the same path I did. Like the home, they'd obviously been there a long time. I tested the large front door, found it unlocked, and walked inside to a small foyer. The house was quiet as a Chick-fil-A on a Sunday morning. The main hallway lead to a door at the back porch visible from where I was standing. To my left, a staircase with a large, ornate newel post led to the second floor. To my right was a community mailbox with four locked sections labeled 1A, 1B, 2A, and 2B, and an open overflow section below for stuff that wouldn't fit in the small locked boxes. I rummaged through the items there and found several sales circulars addressed to Resident and Occupant, a clothing catalog addressed to B. Smith Apt. #1B, and a folded poster promoting a Musician's Corner event at Centennial Park addressed to Cassie Simpshire Apt. #2A. Bingo!

Since no one was around, I decided to walk upstairs and check it out. The stairs creaked a little as I climbed and I ended on a landing partially covered with an old Oriental rug that had seen better days. Next to a window that faced the back of the house was a small table holding a dusty lamp with a faded shade. Apartment 2A was to my left. A doormat shaped like a lotus flower lay outside the door, with the word "Welcome" written in cursive on the white flower's center. The doorknob was a bright new, brushed satin nickel one with a matching deadbolt. I pulled a handkerchief out of my pocket and turned the doorknob. It was locked.

I decided I'd seen enough for this first visit and walked down the short hall to leave, but stopped when I heard a door close and footsteps below. I peeked over the railing and saw a giant of a man carrying a backpack on his shoulders and standing outside the door to 1A. He walked to the foot of the stairs, looked me in the eye and said, "Hey man! Lookin' for somebody?"

Chapter Five

He continued to focus on me as I stopped briefly at the top of the stairs. The guy acted like he might live there, so I took a deep breath trying to calm my racing heart and act my coolest. Then I stepped confidently down the stairs.

"Yep. Comin' down," I said.

When I reached the bottom of the stairs, the guy looked to be a head taller and about a hundred pounds heavier than me. From my place near the door, I figured I could outrun him, if need be. On first pass, he looked to be a nice enough kind of a guy, and I was about to find out.

"My name's Jackson. I'm a PI and I'm doing some work for the construction company across the street. I came by to warn y'all that we might have to blast once in the next hour or so. They didn't want any of the neighbors to hear it and not know what was going on. Bombs goin' off kinda scare folks these days. Know what I mean? So, do you live here?"

"Yeah," he said. "Nice to meet you, Jackson. I'm Michael. I live in 1A." He smiled and stuck out a hand the size of an NFL lineman's, with the grip to go with it.

He continued. "Thanks for the warning about the blast. I'm usually the only one here this time of day and thought you might have been a thief. We had a problem a few weeks ago upstairs, so we're all being extra careful," he said. "We could've used somebody like you around here then."

That explained the new locks on Cassie's apartment.

"If anything ever happens again, feel free to give me a call. Here's my card." I pulled a business card from my wallet, gave it to Michael, and continued my cover story.

"Look, there's still a chance the guys over there won't need to blast if they can dislodge a big rock out back with a backhoe, but it didn't look good this morning. That's why the company got a permit from the city to dynamite it. So then it's my job to make house calls like this and scare the heck out of you neighbors about a potential explosion," I said chuckling, trying to cover my bases in case he got suspicious when the blast didn't happen.

"Any chance your neighbors will be home in the next hour?" I continued.

"Nope. The other dude down here's a salesman and is out of town during the week. He's gone. One apartment upstairs has a couple of singer-songwriters who leave late-morning and don't get back till late at night. They ain't here. The chick upstairs operates like clockwork. She runs or bikes early in the morning, leaves at nine, and gets home around six. Sometimes she goes out at night, but not much. She's out, too. When you live right by the front door like I do, you learn everybody's habits. Folks here kid me about being our security guard, but I'm just a Vandy engineering student that looks like one! So I guess you're done here?"

"Yeah, thanks," I said, not knowing if he was pushing me out the door or in a hurry himself. "I'm going back across the street to see how they're doing. Thanks for your help."

"Sure, man. Anytime," he said as he turned to unlock his door. A deadbolt and doorknob lock were opened with the same key. New hardware; same design as the one I saw upstairs on the door in 2A.

I walked back across the street to my car, then went out behind the house and watched a guy operating a backhoe digging out a place where an outdoor living area might go.

Manuel waved to me and I waved back. After feigning interest as the man dug, scooped and dumped dirt for a few fascinating minutes, I went back to the car and drove to my office.

As I pulled into the parking lot at work, I saw Michelle toss her work bag into the passenger seat of her blue Mazda Miata, complete with bird crap dead center on the hard convertible top. She closed the door, then walked over to me after I parked.

"Have a productive afternoon?" she asked with a look that said she truly was interested in my afternoon.

"Nothing to write home about, but it's a start. Looks like you're knockin' off for the day," I said as I stepped out of the car.

"Yep. Writing all day about paranormal activity in old houses sometimes gets me a little edgy, so I'm ready for a break. Say. Do you have plans for supper tonight? There's a new place just off Twelfth Avenue South that I've been dying to try," she said with a slight toss of her dark brown hair that I found attractive.

"Ah, sure. I'll meet you there, I answered."

"I'll send you a link. It's called the Side B Cafe," she said as she pulled out her phone, typed in some letters and waited for the search to complete.

"Here it is!" she exclaimed. "Give me your number and I'll text it to you."

"That's a great way to get somebody's phone number," I said. "Wish I'd thought of it myself! Of course, the benefit is that I get yours when the text arrives."

She laughed. "And the next time we go out to eat, you'll have my number when you want to send me a link to where *you* want to go. Isn't that convenient?"

"Yes it is, but it assumes you're actually going to enjoy having dinner with me and will want a repeat performance."

"I'll take my chances," she said. "Besides you're probably more entertaining than watching Pat and Vanna on *Wheel of Fortune*, which is what I'll do if I stay at home for dinner."

"You be the judge of that. I'm beginning to think you have an ulterior motive, Michelle," I said, reminding myself that this was the third time we'd had a conversation today and had barely spoken to each other previously.

"Maybe I do, Max. You know, I'm beginning to see why you're good at your job. And I do have an ulterior motive. It involves something I resolved to do on my birthday, the 15th of last month."

"Lemme guess. You resolved to eavesdrop on conversations? Meddle in other people's affairs? Ask almost total strangers to dinner?" I joked.

She laughed. "No, silly. Look. I'm almost 30. I've been in this town for three years and only have four people that I can call good friends. I resolved to get out and meet folks, be active in a church or service organization, and do things that are exciting. Writing about dead people and ghosts all day and only having a few interactions with *real, live people* makes me feel like I'm becoming a hermit. That's why I started going to CoreFitness and how I met Cassie. And by the way, what's up with her?"

"Oh, yeah. Her. Let's talk about that over dinner. Meanwhile, tell me the name of that greasy spoon you wanna go to?"

"The Side B Cafe. It's not a greasy spoon, and I think you'll like it. You know, you still haven't given me your number so I can send you directions."

I called out my number to her while she typed it in her phone. In a few moments, I got a tone notification that a text had arrived.

"How about a quick photo so I can add it to your contact card?" she asked.

"What? Am I that easy to forget? You know what I look like," I answered, getting a wee bit annoyed.

"No. I just like to have photos of contacts in my phone, so when they call, I can see their face and know who's calling. Besides, if you try something you shouldn't tonight, I'll have a recent photo for the police," she said with a little half laugh.

"Believe me. The cops around here already know what I look like. Go ahead and take it fast while I'm still agreeable."

She stepped back, took the photo of her grimacing date and saved it on her phone.

"Let's meet at six. Will that give you enough time to get ready?" she asked.

"I was born ready. And I can't think of anything that would make me late," I answered. Actually, I was pretty excited about dinner together.

Just then, a Metro Police cruiser slowly pulled up the alley and turned into our parking lot. No lights. No siren. Two uniformed cops got out and approached us.

"Good afternoon, officers," I said in a friendly welcome.

"Good afternoon, folks," they both answered. Then one said, "Do either of you know anything about a Maserati that made a stop by here earlier today?"

I leaned over to Michelle and said, "I just thought of something that might make me late."

Chapter Six

*T*he younger of the two officers approached us and said, "One of your neighbors called the station and complained about a Maserati speeding down this alley just after noon. A patrol car cruised the area shortly after the call, but the officers didn't find the car in question. We wrote the complaint off until a half-hour ago, when a car matching the Maserati's description was found wrapped around a telephone pole on Hobbs Road. The driver was dead at the scene."

"Poor guy," I said. "Those cars have a lot of power, and the streets around here are too congested to drive very fast. Had he been drinking?"

"Not sure. Thing is, we don't know what got him first—the pole he ran into or the bullet that got him in the head. None of the airbags were deployed, either."

"Holy crap! He was shot, too?" I said. "Some days aren't worth getting out of bed. And you'd think an eighty-thousand-dollar set of wheels would have reliable air bags."

"You'd think it would, unless somebody tampered with them," said the older of the two officers. He looked at me and cocked his head. "Say, aren't you … Max Jackson? We met at the precinct last year when Sergeant O'Hara had a little conversation with you about a home burglary in a mansion over in Forest Hills."

"Yeah, I remember—a little conversation. I guess you could call it that. I told him what I knew, and fortunately, my client's name stayed out of the papers, and O'Hara got his man. By the way, this is my friend, Michelle McCartney, who works in the office next to mine."

"Nice to meet you, ma'am," he said. "So about the Maserati. Y'all know anything?"

"As a matter of fact, I do. Early this afternoon, I was working in my office. Second floor. You can see the window from here. It's still cracked open. I heard a car pull up, moved my desk chair to look out, and saw the Maserati parked right about where we're standing. Next thing I knew, I heard loud footsteps of someone running up the stairs and then down the hall. A guy bursts into my office, drops a box on my desk, and leaves about as fast and loud as he came."

"Well, that's interesting," the officer said. "Did you get a license number on the car? Can you give us a description of the man and tell us what happened?"

"The license was out of view while the car was parked, and as he drove away, I couldn't see it. The guy was white, tall, late forties or early fifties, long blond hair—he was in bad need of a haircut—and he had a scruffy beard. He wore a black shirt, jeans and cowboy boots. He told me not to follow or look for him and to follow the directions inside the box. Then he vamoosed."

"Okay. So what was in the box?"

"Photos and papers and a jump drive. A lawyer from Atlanta sent me the package and wants me to check up on a gal in town who might inherit a bunch of money from her uncle. If she's clean, she gets the money. If not, it goes somewhere else. I talked to the lawyer this afternoon."

"Interesting. We need you to come down to the station at nine o'clock tomorrow morning, give a statement, and maybe ID the body, Mr. Jackson. Bring the box, too. Here's my card so you can call me if anything else comes up. Oh, would you want to add something, ma'am?" he asked.

"No, nothing at all," Michelle said. "All I heard was a bunch of noise outside in the hallway from my office."

"Okay. Thanks for your time folks. Have a good evening!"

With a tip of their hats, the cops left as quietly as they pulled up: smooth and without fanfare. I thought it was kind of odd since they were investigating a potential murder case. Maybe too many murders makes police and detectives callous. Kind of like surgeons and blood. Lord knows some cops deal with death every day, and it can become old hat. Just another dead body. Just another set of forms to fill out. And if there's a random shooting that has no connection with the killer to the victim, the killer's harder to find, and it ends up being a cold case for the police. I still felt sorry for Mr. Maserati. Even though he was anxious and in a hurry, he didn't let on that he was being chased or in any danger.

"Shot in the head? Oh my stars!" Michelle exclaimed. "I drive down Hobbs when I visit a college roommate of mine. Do you think a madman is on the loose over there? Should I put up the convertible top before the next time I go see her just in case?"

"If it's raining or cold, I would. But I don't think that hard top and glass is going to stop a bullet. All I know is that a delivery guy's dead, and my belly's talking to me. Still wanna get dinner or did you lose your appetite hearin' 'bout a guy gettin' his brains blown out?"

"No, no I'm fine. Instead of meeting there at six, let's go now before it gets too crowded or before I think too much about brains being blown out and what that must have done to the interior of his car. Maybe I *am* thinking about it too much!"

We both drove our cars to Twelfth Avenue and found places to park close to the restaurant's front door. Evidently, Wednesday night wasn't a particularly popular night for eating out—or maybe the restaurant wasn't such a hot place after all. It was located in yet another converted home that went restaurant instead of office building or apartments. A step inside revealed a '60s diner decor, complete with black-and-white checkered tile floor, stools at the counter, and vintage record albums hanging on the wall.

We were greeted by an anxious hipster maitre d'— Brenden, according to his name tag—who dressed head to toe in black, from his Newsie hat to his high-top Cons. He approached us coolly and said, "Welcome to the Side B Cafe! May I ask how many are in your party?"

I looked around, glanced at Michelle, then him, and said, "One, two. Looks like there's two of us. Do you have a booth where two people can have a conversation, sip on a beer, and not be hounded to death by a waiter?"

Michelle glared at me, then looked at Brenden and said, "I'm sorry, sir. My friend's delivery man was shot in the head this afternoon, then he got grilled by the police which delayed us getting here, and he's now hungry. And I've been doing research about old homes in the area just like this one that are haunted with ghosts! It's been a day for both of us!"

"Oh, my! That's awful!" Brenden said with his hand pressed to his chest.

"How about that booth over there?" I pointed toward a back corner of the restaurant near a small stage, complete with a Shure 58 microphone, a couple of acoustic guitars on stands, a cajon, and a Fender Deluxe amp behind them.

"Why, certainly," Brenden answered, giving us a cautious look as he stepped quickly toward our table. We slid into our seats, and he gently placed menus on the table in front of us and said, "Business is kind of slow this evening, so I'll be your server, too. For your dining pleasure, I recommend the Rock and Roll Chicken, which is a fried chicken breast with Ritz cracker and Dijon mustard topping. It comes with Jerry Lee Lewis killer coleslaw. Or there's the Cajun catfish blues dinner—a baked catfish with Louisiana hot sauce and blue-cheese crumbles and herbed steak fries on the side. What may I get you to drink?"

Michelle had been reading the menu while Brenden detailed his dinner recommendations and was already set to give him her order.

"Water for me please, with three slices of lemon. I'll take the strawberry romaine salad and the soup of the day—chicken tortilla, I believe?"

"Yes," Brenden said. "And for you sir?"

"Put me down for the fried chicken and slaw, and pick me out a crisp, dry beer with a funky name that's crafted locally," I said. "Whatcha got for dessert?" I was hoping to save time and get everything ordered in one swoop.

"Our cheesecake and apple crumble are awesome," he suggested.

"They both sound good. How about we get half a slice of each and two plates?" I answered, testing the waters of the "customer is always right" philosophy.

Brenden glanced toward the kitchen area as if looking for approval, and said, "Um… yeah. I guess we could do that. I'll bring it out right after you're finished with the main course. I'll be back with your drinks," he said as he turned to go back to the kitchen. I noticed that Brenden didn't write anything down, but then, there were only two of us, so how hard could it be for him to screw up what we ordered. I figured we'd find out.

"So what did the Kubrick guy tell you?" Michelle asked. "All I could hear was your side of the conversation."

"He said Cassie's rich uncle has an incurable disease and thinks he wants to pass on his inheritance to her, if she's a good kid like he suspects she is," I said. "There are a few other family members in the running, but they're not very well thought of. If none of them work out, the money goes to support bassoonists in the Atlanta Symphony and roses in the botanical gardens. Kubrick and Uncle bucks have a longtime business relationship and Kubrick wants things done to a tee. He needs my job completed in a few weeks, so I'm going to have to get on the ball."

Michelle leaned forward, looking intently at me with her crystal blue eyes and asked, "What are you going to do first? Follow her around town, go to her store, put a bug in her apartment?"

"Well, I checked out her apartment building this afternoon and plan to watch it tonight from across the street. I'm also thinking about visiting her store in the Gulch, but don't know where that'll get me. How she uses her free time will probably reveal the most about her character. Electronic surveillance like bugs are expensive and against the law if you get caught, so that's out."

"It sounds like you could use some help from a clever neighbor who already has an in with her!"

"Why would you want to do something like that?" I answered.

"It would be fun, you know, like I'd be your undercover spy! I could go to her store, go to an aerobics class she was teaching, or have dinner with her. Whatever. If something fishy's going on, I'll tell you. If she's cool, you finish the job, she gets the money, and I get a new friend. What's so hard about that?"

"Not as hard as your head, Michelle. Don't you realize that sometimes lawyers hire a PI like me to investigate someone they suspect of being in trouble or having a problem? This gal might be a real piece of work, and if you do what you say you're going to, you'd be smack right in the middle of it! Who knows? She might try to strangle you with the strings of her running shoes or whatever else she might have around."

Michelle laughed. "My, you don't trust anybody! Whoever heard of using shoelaces as a deadly weapon? But I'll be careful just the same. I can go to her shop tomorrow, look around, and comment on when she taught my class last week. Maybe she and I will get together for coffee or something, too."

Brenden returned and carefully set our plates on the table, except he put my order in front of Michelle, and hers in front of me.

"I think you've got the meals mixed up, partner. I had the chicken," I remarked.

He quickly switched the plates and said, "I am sooo sorry. Sometimes I get all flustered."

"No worries," I said. "And the drinks?"

"Right. The beer. Locally crafted, funky name. And the water! With lemons! I'll be right back."

Brenden scooted back to the kitchen while I, now starving, took the first bite of chicken. It had a nice flavor with a little kick, but not too much. The slaw turned out to be good, too, with a mayonnaise instead of vinegar base.

After a couple of bites, Brenden hustled back to the table out of breath with my beer and Michelle's water in hand.

"Here it is," he announced as he placed the beer next to my plate. "Duck River Brew from southern Middle Tennessee. It's not well-known, but our patrons love it so much the crafters had to increase their production capacity. I hope you enjoy it as well."

He poured Michelle's water from a bottle into an empty glass and said, "And this is mineral water, locally sourced from a spring in Van Leer, Tennessee, where they filter it using double-reverse osmosis, ozonate it, and bottle it for our drinking pleasure."

Brenden picked up the beer bottle, popped the top off, and replaced it on the table. I reached for it, took a swig and said, "That's smooth, Brenden! I can see why it's so popular. Say. Just how does that double-reverse osmosis stuff work on the water?" I asked.

"I am not quite sure," he said, "but it certainly sounds quite impressive, doesn't it." He excused himself from our table, and proceeded to the front door where he greeted another couple who had just arrived.

After a while, we finished our dinner, paid Brenden and promised to come again. On the way out, he mentioned that a three-piece band played there every Friday night and there was always a good crowd. We said we might check it out some time.

Michelle and I left the restaurant and started walking toward our cars.

"Thanks for the dining recommendation, Michelle. That wasn't half bad! Where're you off to next?"

"I'll go back to the apartment and settle down for the night. Might watch a couple of *Downton Abbey* episodes. I've gotten totally hooked on the show and don't know why I didn't watch it when it was new," she said. "Aren't you going to Cassie's tonight?"

"Yep. I plan to stake out near Cassie's till around midnight. Who knows what tomorrow brings, except for the appointment at the police station. Maybe I'll see you at the office in the afternoon. Have a good night!"

Michelle opened her car, then let down the convertible top. I waited to make sure her car started and that she got out of the parking lot okay. It did, then she waved to me, and pulled out on the street winding out first gear, her long brown hair blowing in the wind. I turned on my car's AC and headed home, windows up and hair, for the most part, still in place.

As I approached my home, my octogenarian neighbor Colonel Darrell Canyon called out and greeted me in his usual style.

"Hey there, Sherlock! Solve any mysteries today? Ha!" he laughed and rocked back in his chair.

Then he leaned forward, squinted and scrunched his face and studied mine.

"And why're you wearing that silly smile? You must have had one hot dinner date."

"Hello, Colonel Canyon. Reporting in, sir," I said with a salute. "No mysteries solved today and I did have a dinner date."

"You haven't grinned that much coming home since you did work for that fashion model in Green Hills. You better get inside and throw some cold water on your face before you overheat!"

He laughed again and leaned back in his rocker, then moved his arm quickly and swatted a pesky fly with his fly swatter.

Colonel Canyon was a longtime widower who had served in special forces during his military career. He had an eagle eye, and not much escaped his notice. Frankly, his observation skills were appreciated by our other neighbors; crime on the street was nonexistent since he'd moved in.

When I walked in the house, a "Breaking News" headline from a local TV station popped up on my phone screen. "Gunman Kills Motorist on Hobbs! Details at 10."

I got a feeling that my meeting with the cops tomorrow was going to be a bit more involved than I first imagined.

Chapter Seven

*I*t had been a long day, and was going to be a longer night, but I was glad to have a few minutes to relax on my back porch before heading over to Cassie's. The porch overlooks a creek, which is a nice visual amenity in an area where most homes sit so close together that what people see are backyards with junk lying around. Tall sycamore and water oak trees alongside the creek offered a little privacy from my neighbors. The sound of water cascading over the rocks was very soothing after a busy day. Sometimes I'd just sit and watch the water run, trickling over and around the rocks, and think about nothing at all.

Today, though, I could only think of the events of my crazy afternoon: an intruder bringing me a package; the mysterious guy getting shot; an interrogation by the local police; and the highlight, a visit and dinner with my nice, attractive, and very single office neighbor.

Nine o'clock arrived before I knew it, and it was time to get on the move. I dressed in dark clothes and sneakers, then drove over to Cassie's apartment.

My stakeout spot, the driveway across the street from her place, was vacant because the construction guys had gone for the day. A lone runner wearing earbuds and a Country Music Marathon shirt passed by, lost in his own world, and ignored me as I pulled in the drive and parked around back.

Lights were on in all four apartments at Cassie's place and two cars were parked out front on the street. The hazy summer sky was star-filled and moon-free, with only dim street lights illuminating the scene before me. It was still hot out, so I left the car windows down a little bit in order to not to sweat to death.

I stayed still in the car, occasionally glancing up at Cassie's window and hoping nobody would notice me parked there. Except for a few cars that passed through, the neighborhood was quiet. The only sounds were that of a dog barking, car doors closing, or an occasional owl hoot. This part of town evidently settled in early on a Wednesday night. I sat back in my seat, relaxed but attentive, and got ready for the next two hours to be as bored as a border collie fresh out of Frisbees.

Just as I anticipated, not much happened. Two of the residents in Cassie's place got home around eleven. More lights went on in their second-floor apartment across from Cassie's and stayed on till midnight. Cassie's lights and the others had gone off on both sides of ten o'clock. At midnight, the old home was dark and silent. After fifteen more minutes, I decided my work there was done and drove away slowly, with the car lights off till I got a block away.

The next morning I arrived at work and went to the Happy Bean and Bagel to pick up breakfast. Turns out they made a pretty good sausage, egg and cheese bagel. I added a cinnamon roll; breakfast of champions. That and a cup of French vanilla flavored coffee were just the ticket to get my brain crankin' after a short night's sleep. My buddy, the barista Rohan, handed me the order and took my debit card.

"Anything I need to know before I start work?" I asked.

Rohan had the reputation with shop regulars as the inside news source for race tips, stock recommendations, upcoming arrests—you name it. Nobody knew who his sources were, but he was spot on more often than not.

"Don't bet on horses at Kentucky races this weekend, Max. Bad odds, sloppy tracks with thunderstorms coming tonight. Nice piece of property on Charlotte Pike goes on sale tomorrow, but don't buy it. It has a cemetery with unmarked graves hidden in weeds in backyard that seller doesn't mention," he offered, as if I was some sort of deep pockets developer.

"Thanks for the tips, Rohan. I'll keep 'em in mind."

"Oh! And Ms. McCartney looks very nice today. She's wearing a red dress and a necklace with tiny pearls, and it's not even Friday! What's up with that?" he said with a smile, a lift of the eyebrows and a slight turn of the head.

"Maybe it's too hot for pants," I said, now also curious about Michelle. "Thanks for the breakfast!"

Just as I was leaving, I heard my phone ring. I walked over to a vacant corner of the cafe and set down my sack and coffee on a table.

"Jackson here," I answered.

"Jackson. It's Josef Kubrick from Atlanta. How are things in Nashville today?" he asked in a voice that hinted at news he wanted to tell and that he didn't really care about Nashville but was just making conversation.

"Well, my bagel and coffee are getting cold, I didn't get much sleep last night, and I've got an appointment with a police sergeant this morning, but other than that, nothing special. How 'bout you?"

"Fine, fine. I won't keep you but just a minute. This morning I found out that Sammy Simpshire, Cassie's cousin, was busted on theft at a nice department store in Buckhead last weekend. The police report said he was shopping with somebody and they were looking at men's diamond rings. That somebody was Cassie. According to the clerk, Sammy was trying on several rings that had been placed on the counter. Sammy and Cassie left the store without purchasing anything. Shortly afterwards, the clerk discovered one ring valued at five thousand dollars was missing and alerted security. They found Sammy walking in the mall and took him back to the store where police were waiting for him. The missing ring was in his pocket. Cassie had already left to go to her car. The official report did not list Cassie as a suspect. Sammy said he was innocent and didn't know how the ring got there. Unfortunately, he had a couple of petty thefts on his record, so they took him downtown and booked him."

"So ole Sammy boy's goof-up took him out of the running for the inheritance and landed him in jail. Sorry to hear about that, but thanks for letting me know," I answered.

"Get back to your breakfast and police meeting. You're not in any trouble are you?"

"Nope. Just routine."

"Well, good. Have a good day Jackson."

I made the quick trip up two flights of stairs, unlocked my door and set everything down on the desk. When I finished breakfast, I made a point not to leave my trash out so I could pass inspection from my "housekeeping supervisor" neighbor, Michelle.

The morning was comfortable enough that I raised the window to catch what little cool, fresh morning air I could get. It wouldn't last long with mid-afternoon highs predicted for the upper eighties.

Job one for today was to see what I could find out about Cassie's online. I typed in her name on Facebook and came up empty. Instagram revealed an account, but a private one. Nothing on Twitter or Snapchat either. There were several references to her clothing business—including one in which her company had been a sponsor for a women's run in Nashville—and a photo of her with three guys who were teammates in a collegiate marketing contest her senior year in college. One guy went by the unfortunate name of Mason Dickson.

My watch showed 8:45 which meant it was time for me to head over to the police station. I picked up the box with Cassie's photos and other things in it, and started the five minute walk to see Sergeant O'Hara. I wanted to get there early since the sergeant ran his operation like clockwork and hated people being late.

When I walked into the main lobby, O'Hara was walking down the hallway with another officer. He stopped, smiled, and said, "Jackson! Good to see you! Come on in so we can get started."

I followed him down the hall to his office and sat in a well-worn leather chair near his desk. The other officer continued down the hall.

"Let's cut to the chase, Jackson," he said. "What do you know about this shooting on Hobbs the other day? That's a nice part of town, and folks there don't expect that sort of thing to happen. The Chief of Police wants me to wrap this case up ASAP, so tell me everything you know," he said. He looked at his watch, more or less out of habit. Or maybe he really was in a hurry.

"I'm afraid I'm not going to be much help, O'Hara. It's like I told your boys the other day. The guy ran into my office, told me about the package, and took off. When he walked in, he said he was invisible, that I'd never find him, and not to follow him. He left in such a hurry that I didn't really have a chance to. Later on, I called the office of the lawyers who sent me the package and talked to them about it. They never mentioned the delivery guy; just talked about what they wanted me to do."

"All right. So the box's contents and lawyer call both get at what they want you to do—check out if this woman is a good egg or not, and report back to them. My problem is, why would the delivery guy get shot? Does it have anything to do with the lawyer or the woman in question? Doesn't seem like it would, but maybe. Give me the lawyer's name and phone number. He's got some questions to answer for me."

"Sure." I checked my phone and gave him his name and number. "I've got the address at my office," I said. "I'll send it to you when I get back. What about people in the area where the guy got shot? Anybody suspicious there?"

"There's nothing in our records about criminals living in the area or another crime being committed. Most residents there are retired. There's always a chance it could have been a drive-by shooting, but whoever it was would have to be quite a marksman to shoot a guy driving down the road."

"What about the airbag not going off?" I asked. "Do you think somebody messed with the car?"

"Someone must have," O'Hara replied. "We towed it to the impound lot and have a mechanic examining it now. They said we should know something by this afternoon or tomorrow."

The sergeant glanced at the box in my lap. "I see you brought the box," he said. "Let's take a look at it."

I opened it and showed him the photos, the jump drive, the empty envelope and the note. I told him the jump drive wasn't operable. Nothing else about the box was interesting, but he said he'd keep it as evidence for a few days.

"Would you take a look at the photos of the victim?" the sergeant asked. "Since you were the only one to see him before he got shot, it would be nice if you'd ID him."

O'Hara pulled up a file on his computer and clicked on the photos section. When he found the one he was looking for, he turned the monitor in my direction. I was startled at how gruesome the photo was and tried my best to focus on his features. But something was strange about the picture. The photo was of a fairly young Asian man, smooth-shaven, with black, slicked-back hair. This wasn't the guy who delivered the package!

"Are you sure you've got the right file, O'Hara? That's not the guy that came by my place."

"Yep. It's the right file. I knew the description you gave the officers didn't match this, but I had to check with you to be sure. Could the guy who delivered the package have been a passenger and this one the driver?"

"I doubt it. The white guy who delivered the package jumped in the driver's seat. There might have been someone else hidden in the car, but I didn't see him."

"That's a possibility, or maybe the victim later stole the car from the original driver after he dropped by your place. We found out that the Maserati's VIN number is scratched off, so we can't identify the owner as quickly as usual. Damn, this is just getting more complicated."

O'Hara leaned back in his chair, heaved a sigh and asked, "Well, how's your investigation going?"

"I'm just getting my feet wet, O'Hara, but so far, it looks like this Cassie girl's gonna be a millionaire soon."

"Well, good for her. But if you find anything that has to do with this delivery guy, give me a call. You've got my number," he said as he glanced at his watch again.

I took that to mean that the sergeant was ready to wrap up our conversation and got up to excuse myself.

"Will do, O'Hara. Say, do you still go down to our favorite place, Andy Jack's on 21st?"

"Every now and then. Why?"

"Nothing. I remember we had some good times there a few years ago. And you were quite the expert with darts after a few drinks. Maybe I'll see you there again sometime."

"Maybe so, Jackson. You have a good day now."

I exited the station and started the walk back to my office. I pulled out my phone to see a text from Michelle: *Went to Cassie's store this morning. Got the cutest leggings for wintertime running! :-) But pricey! She's teaching my class tonight. More later!*

I sent her a smiley face response, grateful that she was making progress on getting to know Cassie better.

I arrived at the office close to ten and continued my internet sleuthing. After another half hour of searching, I couldn't pull up anything else of importance, so I decided to go to the gym and work off some energy.

My usual place in the aerobic room was on a stationary bike, third from the end, next to my friend Jacob. His gray Music City Marathon shirt was soaked like he'd taken a shower in it. The guy could sweat like a mule.

"Hey Max! What's up?" he called out in his cheerful tone.

"Not much. You?"

"The usual. Been missin' you here. Where've you been? You used to be a regular," he said, sitting up with hands on his hips and breathing much better than I would if I had ridden as long and hard as he apparently had.

"I've been getting here around six a.m. to beat the crowd. That time of morning I'm usually half-asleep, so my body doesn't realize what I did until I get back home. I'm trying to get in shape for hiking the Smokies this fall."

He laughed.

"Everybody needs a motivator, and hikin's a good one. Mine is my three boys. All three are playin' ball, and it's everything I can do to keep up with them. I think basketball courts have gotten longer since we played in high school," he said, and chuckled again.

Just then, an attractive regular at the gym who wore a gray t-shirt with Everlast written across the front passed by us and stopped at the free-weights rack. She picked up a couple of mid-sized dumbbells and started doing shoulder presses.

Jacob diverted his eyes back from her. "So when are you going to find that special someone and have some kids to play ball with?" he asked. "You're not gettin' any younger, you know. I think Rachel over there is available." He nodded his head back toward the free-weights rack.

"Thanks for pointin' that out, Jacob," I answered. "The time will either come for me to get serious about someone or it won't. Either way, it's fine with me. I actually hope for the former, but just haven't been successful in that department so far. Rachel over there is cute, but finding a woman who can out arm wrestle me isn't necessarily tops on my spousal criteria list."

He chuckled, then leaned forward and started pedaling for all he was worth.

I looked back at Rachel, then thought about my own relationships with women over the past few years. It seemed like whenever I got close to real love, whatever that was, something happened that closed the door on marriage. I guess I was even afraid of opening my life to someone again. One girl I dated several years back broke up with me because she met an old boyfriend at her high school reunion. Sparks between them reignited, and she flew out of my life. Another wasn't enamored with my carrying a gun, keeping odd hours, and sometimes hanging out with despicable characters in bad parts of town. And then, I was engaged a couple of years ago to a beautiful girl who relocated here from Mountain Brook, just outside Birmingham. After a visit to her parents' home, I found out pretty quick that my meager income wouldn't keep her living in the style to which she was accustomed, and that her daddy wouldn't approve. She broke off the engagement, moved back home, and married a coal magnate's son within a year. So much for love.

We cycled a little bit more amid the whir of other cycles, treadmills, and elliptical machines. Jacob's face got a little more serious. "Did you hear about the shooting on Hobbs yesterday?" he asked. "The paper speculated that the car's airbag malfunctioned, too. The whole thing sounds fishy to me."

"Yeah. Fishy for sure," I answered. And he only knew the half of it.

After a good thirty minutes on the bike, I wrapped up my workout, took a shower and headed back to the office. On the way there, I got a call from my client, Greg—the one who was missing his guitar.

"What's up, Greg? Any news on your Martin?"

"My wife said she sold it on Craigslist for $10,000 to a guy in town," he said. "I don't know if he knows what he got or not, but it's a lot more valuable than that. I emailed him about it and told him I wanted it back. He said he sold it to a pawn shop owner downtown for $20,000, but didn't say which one. The guy said he just started buying and selling instruments as a hobby and wasn't a player. He hasn't answered any more of my emails since I got a little hot with him. I guess he figured something was going on since the guitar was so valuable and he'd better lay low."

"Okay. At least I have a lead. I figure not every shop's going to have the kind of money to pay for an instrument like yours. I'll check some of the nice instrument dealers downtown and see if anything comes up. You're ready to pay big-time to get it back, I suppose?"

"Oh yeah! It's just that I hate paying for it twice. I'll probably have to sell something else in my collection to help pay for it. I can do $25,000 tops, even though it's worth about eighty grand."

"Damn! Thanks one fine guitar! I'll let you know what I find out, if anything."

Chapter Eight

*A*s I walked to my office, I noticed that Michelle's office door was ajar and took the liberty to knock and see how she was doing, and maybe check out the red dress Rohan mentioned.

"Michelle?"

"Come in, Max."

She hastily stuffed a small red journal in her top desk drawer and smiled.

Michelle's office was moderately sized like mine with an ergonomic sit/stand desk area separated by a small, L-shaped sectional sofa in a sitting area. That space contained a coffee table, a small flat-screen television mounted on the wall, and a dorm-style refrigerator. Furniture was done in pastels, with nicely framed lithographs of Monet paintings on the wall. The dark wood floor was complemented by natural fiber rugs resting at her work space and under the coffee table. Relaxing acoustic guitar music played from speakers near her desk, and a hint of vanilla aroma wafted by me as I walked in. Michelle turned from her work area and smiled. Rohan was right. Michelle looked dazzling.

"Mornin,' Michelle. I wondered if you'd like to go down to the Gulch with me. I'm working on another case and need to visit a pawn shop there. I thought you could show me Cassie's place while we're in the neighborhood."

"Sure! Let me wrap up this last email and I'll be right with you."

She typed a few more keystrokes on her Mac, hit the send button, and shut it down. She walked over to me, looked at her watch and said, "How about we grab lunch while we're there?"

She picked up her purse, threw the strap over her shoulder, then locked and closed the door as we exited.

On our way there, Michelle told me about her shopping adventure at Cassie's and how nice all her merchandise was. She said there weren't many customers, and figured mornings were probably her slow times. Michelle was very excited about Cassie teaching class that night.

When we arrived in the Gulch, I found the last spot in a "pay the machine after you park" parking lot. The machine only took credit cards and ten-dollar bills, which said a lot about how valuable parking spaces were downtown. I fed the machine my credit card and secured two hours of ticket-free parking in space twenty-three, Michael Jordan's number.

We walked over to a street-level sandwich shop with indoor and outdoor seating. The management there was smart enough to have a few of the more popular sandwiches freshly prepped and available for sale in the refrigerator so everyone didn't have to order at the counter. We took advantage of the fast track, and did self check-out just like the grocery store without having to speak to a soul.

Michelle found a raised table with tall stools near the front window where we could enjoy the view of cars and pedestrians traveling up and down Twelfth Avenue South, and a giant yellow crane lifting steel to build yet another high-rise. People who lived in this part of downtown said that there's just something about the Gulch. I was one among many who hadn't yet discovered what that something was.

"So, how did your morning go at the station, Max?" she asked.

"Fine," I said. "I explained everything to O'Hara, and he showed me a photo of the guy who was shot in the car."

"Oh, I bet that was gross! Why did he do that?"

"He wanted me to ID the guy, and yes, it was a pretty gruesome photo. But the big news is that he's not the same guy who delivered the package to me! Our guy was a fortyish white dude. The guy shot in the car was younger and Asian. They were still tryin' to find out who he was, but hadn't yet. O'Hara's going to call Mr. Kubrick in Atlanta and see what he knows. I think we're out of it for now unless Cassie's involved in it somehow. But I doubt that."

"So you're saying that the guy who delivered the package has disappeared and they don't know who was shot in the car?" Michelle said. "This is getting stranger by the minute, Max."

"Sure is, Michelle. The VIN number was scratched off the car and there weren't any identification papers in the glove compartment. Must have been stolen. The cops will probably find the owner, though, since there aren't that many Ghiblis around."

We finished lunch and walked a couple of blocks down to Beauregard's 12th Avenue Pawn. The sign—"*We specialize in the finest of musical instruments and jewelry*"—made me hope I'd found the home for Greg's guitar. When we walked in, I was impressed. It may have been the nicest pawn shop I'd ever been to. Everything was neatly arranged with price tags visible, and all the chrome and glass cases shined like they were ready for inspection by a manager from Tiffany's.

"Welcome to Beauregard's Pawn Shop!" boomed a short, squatty man wearing an untucked flowered shirt that barely covered his substantial beer belly. He brushed back a few lonely hairs from his comb-over and said, "I'm Beauregard. What can I interest you in today? Perhaps something for the little lady?"

Even though he was addressing the both of us, Beauregard primarily eyed Michelle, giving her the once-over two or three times. She wandered toward the jewelry counter as I approached the proprietor. That look on her face showed she didn't appreciate the "little lady" comment.

"Howdy, Beauregard. I'm Max. I'm trying to find a nice guitar," I told him. "Something special," I added.

"Just how nice would you like, Mr. Max? We have all makes, models and prices."

"How about a late '30s Martin, triple-aught 45 with double bound Abalone trim."

"That certainly would be special, Max! Maybe one with an Adirondack spruce top and Brazilian rosewood back and sides?"

"Yeah. And a 14-fret mahogany neck; ebony-bound fretboard with inlay, ebony bridge, and rosewood bridge plate?"

"What if it had a Brazilian rosewood headstock, Grover open gear tuners, and came in the original hardshell case? One like that?" he said with a glimmer in his eye, and rubbing his hands together as if he were warming them or praying or anticipating a major sale.

"You bet. A client of mine's angry wife sold his guitar with that exact description without his knowledge. He'd like to get it back. I understand it's pretty valuable."

"Very valuable, and good luck findin' one," he said as he turned, and started to walk back to the counter.

In a moment, he stopped, turned back to me and started laughing.

"I'm messin' with you, Mr. Max. It just so happens that I bought a guitar like that from a rookie collector the other day. The doofus obviously didn't know what it was worth, and took $20,000 for it. I asked him where he got it, afraid it might have been stolen, and he gave me the same story you did about the wife. I could have sold it to a big-time collector friend of mine, but kind of figured that it was somebody's baby and decided to hold on to it for a while. I used to play guitar and have regretted selling any of my old instruments. Once, while I was on tour, somebody stole one I particularly loved, and I never saw it again."

"Mind if I see the guitar and text a photo to my client? It sounds like the one he's looking for."

"No problem. It's in the safe. I'll go fetch it."

Beauregard went to a back room and shortly returned with the instrument in question. As he carefully opened the case, the aroma of old guitar in an old case—whatever that's called—filled my senses. It reminded me of how my Aunt Ruby's parlor, filled with antique furniture and books, smelled when I visited there as a kid.

I took a photo and texted it to Greg, hoping he wasn't busy and could confirm that we had the right instrument. Greg got it and asked to see a photo of the back; there was a small belt-buckle scratch near the base of the body on his. Sure enough, there it was. He asked to speak to the current owner and I handed him my phone.

After some head shaking and nodding from Beauregard as the two negotiated prices, Beauregard handed the phone back to me.

"Well, we've got a deal. This beauty will be back in his rightful owner's hands tonight."

I asked him: "I know it's none of my business, but do you mind tellin' me what y'all decided on? I know that six-string's worth a ton of money."

"It is that," he said. "We settled on $25,000, which is way below what I could have gotten for it. The thing is, I make a few bucks on the transaction, I'm sure you'll get your commission, and a fellow picker gets his baby back. I'd say that makes it a good day."

"You know something, Beauregard? You're a decent guy. Not everyone would do business like that. It was nice meetin' you."

"Same here." He turned and looked Michelle's way again.

"It looks like your lady friend has an interest in the diamond rings. Is she someone special?" he said in almost a whisper.

"Well, it's just that .... well, we're friends. I don't know about the special part."

"Well if she's not, then I might see if she has any plans for the evening."

I felt my hackles rise a bit. "I wouldn't bother—she's just in town for a seminar. She's taking over the family business in Seattle and needs some extra training." I didn't know where that whopper came from, but I hoped it let him know she wasn't available. And Seattle was very far away. So there.

"Seattle, huh," he said. "That's a long way even for a long-distance relationship."

"Yep." I agreed. "Damn long way."

Michelle called out from a counter nearby and said, "Max. Come look at all these diamond engagement rings."

I walked over to her and spied the rings in the glass cabinet in front of her.

She sighed. "There must be a hundred stories about why these rings ended up for sale in a pawn shop. I bet most of them are tragic since they're not on some girl's finger right now. She gets engaged, something happens, they break off the engagement, and the ring ends up here through no fault of its own. It's like they're all laid to rest in a graveyard of relationships. So sad."

"I guess that's one way to look at it," I said, trying to avoid waxing philosophical about pawned jewelry. "Maybe they just traded up for a bigger diamond. Or even worse—a guitar," I offered.

"Maybe. But still…" she trailed off still in pensive thought about the rings.

"Thanks again, Beauregard," I said, and waved to him as we left the store.

Once outside, I asked Michelle, "How about you take me to Cassie's shop? Isn't it nearby?"

"Sure, but don't you think she'll get suspicious if I come by for a second time today?"

"You're probably right. Let's just pass by it so I can see it, then we'll head back to the office." We strolled down the sidewalk in the direction of Cassie's shop.

Michelle said softly, "I heard what you told that guy about me being from Seattle. Where'd that nonsense come from?" she asked with a smile.

"Good ole Beauregard was checking you out too much and getting a little nosy for my taste, so I thought that fish tale might pour cold water on his plans. It's all I could think of at the moment."

"Max. I'm perfectly capable of taking care of myself," she said with indignation in her voice. "I'm a grown woman with a black belt in Taekwondo, and I'm careful about the people I hang around with."

"Evidently you're not too careful. You've been hanging around a bum like me who you've only known for the last two days, and now you're joining me to play junior detective," I said.

"Maybe I find you interesting, Max. I can't say you're a charmer, but you are interesting."

She laughed and I grinned.

"Look! We're almost at Cassie's shop," she said. "It's right here with the red-and-white striped awning and the rack of clothes out front."

Suddenly, the door to the shop opened and out stepped an attractive young woman dressed for a lunchtime run. She turned, looked at us, and said in a perky voice, "Hi, Michelle! Twice in the same day! Who's your friend?"

Chapter Nine

"**H**i, Cassie! This is Max Jackson. He works in the office next to mine."

"Cool. Nice to meet you, Max. Look y'all, I'm supposed to join someone a couple of blocks away in a few minutes, so I'd better get going," she said all while running in place.

"You go on. I'll see you in class tonight," Michelle said as she waved to her friend, turning to run down the street.

"Isn't she nice?" said Michelle.

"Seems so," I answered.

As we walked back to the car and drove to our office building, Michelle told me about her college days and what brought her to Nashville. She put herself through Samford University in Birmingham, had a partial swimming scholarship and worked as a waitress some evenings and weekends. She caught the writing bug covering swim events for the school paper, *Bulldog Bites,* and decided to make a career of it. A now-defunct Nashville newspaper gave her her first real job as a features writer doing stories on odd happenings about town. Another draw was a now ex-boyfriend, who had since been lured away from her by a swim teammate whose long blond hair, brown eyes and yellow Corvette convertible struck his fancy. Michelle still hated Vettes, she told me. And convertibles. And blondes with brown eyes, but she laughed and said she was kidding about that. I told her she was lucky to lose him and to get over the car thing. It wasn't the Corvette's fault.

Back at the office, I picked up some papers and headed back to the house. Tonight was night two on stakeout, and I wanted to get a little rest so I could resist going to sleep sitting in the car waiting for something to happen which probably wouldn't.

Nine o'clock finally arrived—time for me to resume my post across from Cassie's place. Much like last night, there wasn't much activity, but there were definitely more cars passing down the street. With my windows down, I could hear a band playing in the distance from a nearby restaurant with a rooftop bar.

Close to ten o'clock, I spotted a wandering dog of no particular denomination who sauntered by the front yard at Cassie's home, stopping to sniff and then pee near a bush where, I assumed, another dog had left a message. From my vantage point, it looked like it wore a collar, so I expected his owner wasn't far behind. Sure enough, a guy followed shortly and whistled for the dog to stop, and he did so right in front of Cassie's apartments.

The guy walked over to the dog and stopped under a large oak tree near the stone footpath to the front porch. I slowly eased down in the seat to a point where I was out of view but still able to take in the scene unfolding below. The guy looked around, texted something on his phone, then looked up toward the front window of Cassie's apartment. A light went off in her front room, and Cassie appeared at the front porch of the house shortly after. She walked toward the man and got a thorough sniff-down from the dog, who, not getting a pat out of it, moved on for other adventures in the yard. The two humans greeted each other and appeared to talk about something, but I couldn't make out what. Then he reached in his back pocket, pulled out a small envelope and handed it to Cassie. She took the envelope and gave him a similar one, appeared to say thanks, turned, then made her way back inside. The transaction was completed in a New York minute. The guy and his dog continued down the street just as nonchalantly as they arrived. Moments later, the front room light switched back on in Cassie's apartment.

Now what the heck was that all about? I wondered. I figured nothing else would happen at Cassie's, so I decided to tail the guy and his dog—as much as I could anyway—and see what I could find out. No cars were coming, so I pulled out of the driveway quietly, with the lights off, slowly driving the direction he was walking. I tried to keep a thirty-to forty-yard distance between the two of us so I wouldn't be noticed.

The guy and his dog turned right at the first street, then left at the next, almost making me think he was going in a zig-zag pattern on purpose. He stopped at the third intersection and took out his phone, texted a short message and replaced the phone in his back pants pocket. By then, I had caught up with him and turned on my car lights which startled him.

I lowered the passenger-side window, pulled up to the stop sign close to the curb, and called out, "Hey! You in the blue shirt! I happened to be parked a couple of blocks back doing neighborhood watch, and noticed you and a woman exchanging envelopes. You wouldn't happen to be dealing drugs, would you? We don't cotton to that kind of activity around here."

He toughened up. "What are you? Some kind of cop? It's no business of yours what we did."

The guy favored one of the men in the photo with Cassie that I'd seen recently. I held up my cell phone and said, "I'm makin' it my business, bubba. And with one push of this button I can make it my friend Detective Pate's business, too. He can be down here in three minutes. What'll it be—me or the cops? You've got five seconds!"

"No, no! Don't call the cops! Honest! I'm not dealin' drugs or doing anything wrong!"

The tone of his voice radically changed, and he started to look nervous. I put down the phone and looked him in the eye.

"Okay, then. Tell me what's going on. If it wasn't drugs, what *was* in the envelopes?"

He moved closer to the car, leaning down to the window and said, "Look buddy. They were letters - just letters. I gave her one from her boyfriend, Mason, who lives in Atlanta. She gave me one to mail back to him. Mason and I were friends at Belmont; he and Cassie started dating our senior year. Her dad didn't and still doesn't approve of Mason and forbids her to have anything to do with him. Cassie's dad is a serious techie, and she's afraid that with his know-how, he could stalk her email account and text messages. So that's why she and Mason communicate by letters sent to my address. They're too paranoid to mail a letter directly to each other."

"So these two think her old man can hijack the U.S. Postal Service and cell phones?" I asked.

"He probably can't, but they don't want to take any chances," he answered.

"Ever read one of them?" I asked.

"No way! What do you think I am? Whatever they write is their business. He writes about twice a week, mails it to me, I get it to her, and then vice versa. I guess it's kind of like Romeo and Juliet."

"Let's just hope there's no dagger and poison involved," I said. "All right, dude, I'm going to leave you alone. But I'd advise you to find a less suspicious way to swap letters. The next neighborhood watch guy might not be so understanding. Adios!"

I closed the window and peeled out, turning right from the intersection leaving the guy standing at the corner, drop-jawed. He still looked shocked, so much so that he didn't even reach for his cell phone for whatever comfort that might have given him. I decided to call it a night and continued home.

Chapter Ten

A few hours later, I was jerked out of that crazy dream about totally forgetting a class one semester in college by the sound of my phone vibrating on the nightstand. The clock showed it was two in the morning. I grabbed the phone and sat up quickly when I saw that Michelle was calling.

"Hey, Michelle! What's the matter?"

"I'm in the emergency room at Vanderbilt Hospital," she answered softly.

"What happened? Were you in a wreck?" I tried to shake myself out of my sleep-deprived brain fog.

"No—it's kind of a complicated story, and I'm not sure if I've got it all straight myself. They're about to release me, but the doctor says I can't drive home. Would you be so kind as to come get me?"

"Absolutely! Give me fifteen minutes."

I hung up without even saying goodbye and set the phone down, threw some water on my face, got dressed like I was fleeing a house fire, and then ran outside to the car. My mind was racing, worrying about what was up with Michelle. She said it was a complicated story and wasn't allowed to drive. Her speech was rational, although she sounded tired; it probably wasn't a head injury. I knew she went to Cassie's Zumba class last night. And I saw Cassie around eleven, meaning she wasn't with Michelle when it happened, whatever it was.

At this hour of the morning, traffic to Vanderbilt University Medical Center was a piece of cake, unlike almost any other time of the day. When I arrived, I found an area designated "Emergency Patient and Family Parking Only - Violators will be Towed," whipped into a parking place, and walked briskly toward the ER entrance.

Once inside, I saw thirty or forty people—some curled up on couches sleeping, some sitting in small groups, and several sitting alone with a look of concern on their faces for whatever was going on behind the door that led to the patient-care area. I couldn't help but feel sorry for them and wonder about the fate of whomever they were here to see, but I was mainly concerned about Michelle. I spotted the information desk and made a beeline to speak to the receptionist.

"May I help you, honey?" the smiling woman behind the glass partition asked me with a gravelly voice obviously affected by many years of smoking.

"I'm here to see Michelle McCartney. She just called me and said she was about to be discharged, but needed a ride home. Is she okay?"

Agnes, (according to her name tag) placed her reading glasses on the tip of her nose and typed something into her computer. She pulled a pencil from her permed gray hair and used it as a pointer on her computer screen.

"You'll have to ask the nurse about her condition, but I can tell you she's in 13A in the Fast Track area. Now if she was hurt bad, she'd be in trauma, but mind you, I can't give out patient health information. I'll call her nurse and let her know you're here," she said, with a wink.

Just as she picked up the phone, a nurse came out through the authorized area doors pushing an elderly gentleman who had a large, clean white bandage on his forehead. Three people standing nearby came to meet them at the door and followed the nurse to a car waiting just outside.

"Katrina!" Agnes almost shouted as the nurse returned from outside with the empty wheelchair. "This here man was called by 13A to come pick her up. Would you mind taking him back?"

I approached the nurse and introduced myself. "I'm Max Jackson. Michelle called me and asked if I could pick her up here. How's she doin'?"

Katrina's crystal blue eyes complimented her deep blue scrubs, and her confident smile and composure made me feel better even before her report on Michelle.

"She'll be fine," she said. "Just needed some fluid and electrolytes. Follow me and we'll go see her."

The double doors opened, prompted by her badge scan, and we walked into an area hectic with medical devices beeping, staff on phone calls, and nurses zipping around. We walked a short distance down the Fast Track hall to tiny room 13A and found Michelle sitting up in a chair, dressed and ready to go. She forced a smile, but with her already fair complexion, she looked as pale as if she'd just donated a pint too many at the Red Cross.

"Max! You made it!" She slowly stood to rise and embraced me in a hug that was a little more than just "I'm glad to see you." I held her gently, glad she was okay, and asked, "How are you feeling?"

"Better now. They gave me some IV fluids and I perked up in no time. I still don't know why they won't let me drive home." She slowly sat back down in the chair as if she were still a little woozy.

Katrina chimed in. "I can think of two reasons why you can't drive home. One: You just came into an emergency room and passed out. Two: Someone else brought you here in their car, and I have no idea where yours is." She smiled. "Now, you rest here for a few more minutes. I'll be monitoring your blood pressure from the nurses' station. The doctor has written to release you in about five minutes if it's WNL—that is, within normal limits."

She gently touched Michelle on the shoulder and walked out of the room. I sat in a chair facing her and said, "Tell me what happened. Who brought you here? Has anything like this happened to you before?"

"Hold on, Max! One question at a time." She sat in the chair, tilted her head back, and looked up at the ceiling as if searching for an answer.

"I had just left Cassie's place. We had an incredible workout at her Zumba class, and she invited me over for coffee afterwards. I don't usually have coffee at night, but it seemed like a good idea at the time. We talked and talked, and I left there about ten. On the drive home, I started feeling faint, so I pulled over and parked. Then I felt nauseous and dizzy and got out of the car. The next thing I knew, I was lying on this stretcher, here in the emergency room with an IV in my arm and a couple of nurses hovering over me. Not knowing where I was and waking up like that kind of freaked me out till I got oriented."

"So how *did* you get here?" I asked.

"They told me that a Lyft driver brought me. A guy named Jerry. He was driving by and said he saw me get out of my car, stumble, and watched me fall and pass out on the sidewalk. He picked me up, put me in his car and brought me here. He was quick-thinking enough to get my purse and keys out of the car and bring them with him since he didn't know who I was or what was going on. Said he used to work here, and he figured I'd get help quicker by bringing me here instead of calling an ambulance. Besides, I was only a few blocks away."

"And where is he now?"

"He stayed till I regained consciousness and saw that I was all right, then had to go on a Lyft run. He left me his card. That guy was really nice to go out of his way to help."

"A good Samaritan," I said, thankful that such folks were still out there.

About that time, nurse Katrina pulled back the curtain and entered our tight space carrying some papers.

"The monitor shows that your blood pressure is about right, so it's time to get you out of here. Just sign these papers and we'll escort you to the door." She handed one to me. "And you need to sign this paper saying you're taking her home."

I took the paper, signed my name and gave it back to her.

"I'll pull my car up and wait for you out front, Michelle," I said as I exited the treatment area. Just as I stuck my head outside the curtain, I had to stop suddenly for a group of ER staff rushing by pushing a gurney with a patient obviously in pain, with blood covering his face and arms. When the path cleared, I headed out of the ER to the parking lot.

As I pulled up to the door, I saw Katrina pushing Michelle in a wheelchair. Michelle stood with ease this time, walked to the car, and settled in the passenger seat.

"Stay well-hydrated for the next twenty-four hours," Katrina said. "You're a lucky woman, Michelle, with two men willing to take care of you on the same night. Not all of our patients are so fortunate. Some people just get left on the street for the cops to get them. Take care." And with that, gently closed the car door.

Michelle reached over and held my arm. She looked at me. "I am a lucky woman," she said. "Thanks for coming to my rescue, Max."

I pulled out of the patient pick-up area and pointed the Altima toward 21st Avenue. "You're welcome, Michelle. Now you're going to have to tell me where you live so I can fulfill my obligation with the hospital."

Michelle pointed in the general direction of 21st Avenue and said, "Sure. It's easy. Take a right, then left at the next big intersection. Go straight for five blocks, turn right, and I'm the second driveway on the right. The number 203 is on the mailbox."

"Got it. I'm still curious, Michelle. What do you think caused you to pass out? Do you have some kind of medical condition?"

"No. But the doctor figured out what happened. He said that I was dehydrated."

"I know you went to Cassie's Zumba class, which would cause you to sweat, but that shouldn't have been enough exercise to cause this kind of problem. Should it?"

"No. According to the doctor, the problem was compounded by the coffee I had later at Cassie's apartment. The caffeine made me pee, so I lost more water and electrolytes."

"She didn't offer you Gatorade or something after your workout?"

"No."

"So what happened next?" I asked.

"Well, we were talking girl stuff, and I told her I'd been feeling crampy because it was that time of the month for me, so she gave me a pill that she uses for the same thing—something thiazide."

"Michelle! That's a pill for blood pressure! My dad takes it! It causes people to urinate more, and they lose sodium and potassium in the process. What with that exercise class, caffeine in the coffee and a water pill, it's no wonder you got dehydrated! Hell, you could have died!"

"Yeah. That's what the doctor said, too," said Michelle, dropping her eyes and head in embarrassment.

After passing through several intersections and a right turn, I found house number 203. I turned into the driveway and stopped for a large black wrought iron security gate blocking the entrance. A slightly shorter fence also sealed off the front yard from the street.

"Put in the code 257 and a pound sign, then the gate will open," Michelle directed.

I punched in the code and the gate opened to reveal a pea gravel driveway with a tall, thick bamboo forest of green screening her place from the neighbor on the left and a tall, ivy-covered brick wall doing the same on the right. Despite the homes being close, the view of neighbors on either side were obscured. From what I could see in the headlights, Michelle's backyard was a miniature Eden dominated by a couple of large oaks shading ferns and a host of hostas. A naked female concrete nymph, spot-lit, poured a never-ending supply of water from an urn into a heart-shaped pool near the back door. A similar naked male sculpture stood nearby watching with great interest.

"Nice place you have here. I didn't know writing about ghosts paid so well," I remarked.

"It doesn't, but going to a party where they gave out lottery tickets as party favors certainly did. That's a long story that I'll tell you later. Speaking of stories, you won't believe what I saw at Cassie's apartment!"

Michelle punched in the same 257 code on the back door lock and ushered me into a cheerful kitchen done in tasteful shades of gray with small bursts of red sprinkled throughout. But at this hour of the morning, it was a little too cheery for me. She led me to the den and promptly plopped down on a couch and placed her head on one of the many pillows tossed about.

"I bet you could use some rest, Michelle. You've had quite a night!" I said, thinking she hadn't had much sleep tonight— unless you count being passed out "sleep."

"I have, and I do need a rest. But listen to what I found out! While I was at Cassie's, we talked about everything; family, work, music, guys, living single in Nashville—you name it. She did mention her somewhat dysfunctional family. Her dad has always meddled in her business and doesn't like her boyfriend. Her Mom is very submissive and takes her dad's side in arguments, never taking up for Cassie. Mason, her boyfriend, has a good job as a supervisor at a clinical reference lab in Atlanta, but that's not prestigious enough for her dad."

"How about that! What else?" So far, Michelle's findings matched my own.

"She had these letters on the kitchen table...."

Chapter Eleven

"**L**etters? What kind of letters?" I asked anxiously.

"Listen and I'll tell you. So we were sitting at her kitchen table drinking coffee and eating rice cakes when Cassie excused herself to go to the bathroom. I guess because she owns a store and is out a lot, she doesn't make time to keep a neat apartment. She had an elaborate kitchen so I figured she liked to cook— probably lots of healthy stuff. There was even a recipe card on the card for poppy-seed chicken on the table with a sticky note that said 'make for Gabriel.' Stuff was everywhere! Her apartment wouldn't get the *Good Housekeeping* Seal of Approval. Anyway, on the kitchen table were some *handwritten letters*, open, and just lying there, right in front of me. I was curious about them, since I hardly ever get a real, handwritten letter. For some reason, I reached for the one on top and began to read it. It was dated a couple of weeks ago and was signed by Mason. In one of the few paragraphs I read, he said his lab had just done a pathology report on her uncle, Claude Deere, whom Mason remembered meeting a couple of years ago. Since Mr. Deere was family, Mason figured Cassie already knew about his cancer and wrote to say he was sorry. He said that the prognosis for this type of cancer wasn't very promising, and that he probably didn't have long to live."

"So the family secret is out! Cassie knows about her uncle's cancer. I wonder what she'll do with that information. And to boot, boyfriend Mason just committed a major HIPPA violation."

"There's more to the story," Michelle said. "When Cassie came back from the bathroom, she saw me looking at the letter and said, 'What are you doing?' in a raised voice. I put it down as quickly as I could. I told her that I hadn't seen a letter written by hand in forever, and noticed that Mason wrote it. I commented that he had nice handwriting for a guy. She hurriedly gathered all of the letters on the table in a messy pile and took them back to her bedroom. When she returned to the kitchen, she put her hands on her hips and said she was supposed to meet someone soon, and that I'd better be going. Cassie was more than a little put out. Close to mad! Max, I really like Cassie. I hope this won't hurt our friendship. Anyway, that's when she gave me the pill to help with my cramps. She said it helped her when she took them."

"Michelle! Don't you know you should never take another person's prescription medicines? Why it could … well, I guess you know from personal experience what could happen," I said, wondering if this woman had one lick of common sense, and also wondering if Cassie knew what she was doing when she shared the pill.

"And then?" I asked.

"She quickly walked to the front door and motioned her hand toward the outside hallway. Then she said, 'I guess you'll be going now.' So I picked up my things and walked to the door. I told her that I had a good time with her tonight and was sorry I read her mail. She shrugged it off and said they were kind of personal and that she didn't appreciate me looking at them, but also that she was in a hurry to meet somebody really soon and didn't want to be late. She was for sure anxious either to get me out of the apartment or to meet whoever it was. Or both."

It occurred to me that the next appointment on Cassie's calendar that evening was with her personal mailman.

Then Michelle tucked up her legs, settled into the pillow and closed her eyes. She kept speaking, although this time in a softer voice, almost like she was talking in her sleep.

"I remember going out to my car feeling a little dizzy but not that bad," she said. "Then I…"

Michelle's voice trailed off, and then she lay there very still. Silent. Exhaustion from her exhausting evening had finally set in. Draped on a wing chair nearby was a thin pink-and-white blanket, which looked just right to keep her warm from the cool of the air conditioner. I gently placed it to cover her waist and legs. I turned off a nearby lamp, which made the room almost dark except for the soft yellow glow of streetlights outside peeking in through the blinds. And for some reason, I gave her a gentle kiss on the forehead and whispered goodnight.

I debated whether or not to stay, but decided it would be best to let Michelle rest alone. The poor woman had had one heck of a day what with a full day's work, a tough workout, a good time with a friend—except for what happened at the end of the visit—and a medical event that landed her in the emergency room.

As I turned the doorknob to leave, I heard a buzz and saw a light coming from where Michelle had placed her cell phone. I looked at it, wondering who would be contacting her at this time of the morning. The text message read, *"Where R U? Tried to call this evening, but didn't hear back. U OK? Call me."* The name at the top of the message identified the text was from Evan—no photo, strangely enough—and it looked like there were several other messages from him prior to this one, but I didn't read them. Who was this Evan guy? Family? Friend? Somebody special?

On the drive home, I had a million thoughts racing through my own sleep-deprived brain. Three hours didn't provide me enough REM sleep to think clearly. Thoughts mainly revolved around Michelle, whom I mentally pictured sleeping on her couch. I worried about this interesting, free-spirited, fun woman who was a bit naive. Wasn't she aware of what was happening to her that night? Did Cassie purposely plan for Michelle to be in that condition or were they both clueless? Was there something else in the letters that Cassie thought Michelle had seen, and, if so, what was it? Did Michelle omit telling me something she saw in the letters in an effort to cover for Cassie? Was Cassie out for Michelle now or would they stay friends? If Cassie *was* out for Michelle, I had a much bigger problem on my hands than whether she was worthy of a big inheritance. I sure didn't want to put Michelle in harm's way for one of my cases. And it still bugged me: Who the heck was Evan?!!

My internal alarm clock woke me at six-thirty the next morning despite the fact that I only had a couple of three-hour sleep sessions in the past twelve. Dawn's early light streaming through a high window in the bedroom coupled with the sound of an ambitious neighbor and his lawn mower roaring outside made it impossible to go back to sleep anyway.

I usually spent time Saturday mornings tidying up my place and this Saturday was no exception. I wasn't expecting any company, not that I ever had company, but I liked for things to be neat and in order. Afterwards, I persuaded myself to get out and decided to drive over to the park and run a few laps before it got too hot outside. After a cup of coffee, of course, and maybe a quick glance at the paper to see if there was a story about the Maserati guy's murder.

When I arrived at the park, I noticed there was a race in progress, though most runners had already completed the course. A few stragglers made the most of the last ten yards and put everything they had into finishing with a bang. After a while, the last runner, an old man hunched over while he ran, fighting for every step and breath, passed over the finish line to the cheers of the few left hanging around for the race to end. Shortly afterwards, race officials quickly began to dismantle timing gear, flags, and other race paraphernalia under the watchful eye of Metro Police, who were anxious to get the roads reopened.

Vendors started to pull into the area with trucks to load their wares and displays. It was then that I noticed a booth for Winner's Threads—Cassie's store. I watched as Cassie stuffed clothes in large tote boxes then loaded them in the backseat of a black, late-model Ford F-150 Raptor with a Georgia license plate. The Winner's Threads banner was untied from support poles, then rolled up and placed in the truck bed. A burly helper carried the heavy metal support poles to the truck bed and secured them with bungee cords since they were a couple of feet longer than the bed, even with the tailgate down. Once everything was loaded, Cassie and her big friend climbed aboard the truck. A nearby policeman blew his whistle in their general direction and motioned for them to come his way, then down an alley to avoid oncoming traffic. The last three vendors were almost done with their packing, which would allow for traffic on the street to get back to normal.

After a quick sprint to my car, I fired it up and pointed it in the same direction they drove. The cop motioned me through, but also mouthed "slow down" and gave me the look as I passed by. I spotted the big truck turn up ahead, and made a point to stay a block or so back so they wouldn't see me following them.

They drove leisurely and took a turn onto I-65 South toward Franklin, and after several miles, pulled off at the exit ramp for Moore's Lane. I was still five or six vehicles behind them and hopefully out of sight. They took the second right at a BP station and proceeded down the road. All the cars in front of me went straight, so I had to back off a little.

I hadn't been on this road in forever and soon discovered that several high-end car dealerships had opened since the last time I'd been here: There were new Alfa Romeo, Aston Martin, and Rolls Royce dealerships ... to name just a few. Eventually, they pulled into the Porsche dealership, got out of the truck and approached the showroom. I kept on driving and found myself at a dead end, where I turned around. What the heck was a woman living in a small apartment who owned what looked to be a struggling business doing at a Porsche dealership? And who was the mystery guy with her?

I couldn't find a place where I could casually park my car and kill time while they shopped, so I just drove around the nearby mall area and planned to be back in ten or fifteen minutes to see what was next on their agenda. After the time passed, I drove by the Porsche place and saw the truck pulling out just as I got there. I turned my head away from them so they wouldn't see me, then sped to the end of the street, made a U-turn and hit the gas trying to catch them.

They turned left at the light, but I was too far behind them to make the green light, too. I figured that they had to go to Cassie's store or apartment next to unload, so when the light finally turned green, I took a chance and went in the direction of her apartment. It must have been my lucky day because there they were, back at her apartment, starting to unpack the truck. I parked in my surveillance spot across the street at the home construction site, surprised that workers weren't there on Saturday. When it looked like the truck was empty, I got out of the car and walked across the street toward the apartment.

The coast looked clear, so I crept quietly around the back of the house and approached the large truck that was jacked up so high most people would need a stepladder to get in. I should have taken a hint when I read the two bumper stickers on the back bumper: *Protected by Smith and Wesson* and *Just because you're offended doesn't mean you're right!* I tiptoed around to the passenger side and noticed the window was down. As I reached for the door handle to pull myself up and look in, I heard footsteps in the gravel and an angry voice coming from the front of the truck. "Hey! What are you doin'?" I jumped down quickly, but before I could turn to get a look at who was yelling, he grabbed my arm in a hammerlock and smashed my head into the side of the truck just missing the door handle. I felt a sharp pain in my arm, then on my forehead as my head slammed into the door. I remember looking briefly up to the sky and then my whole body went limp and everything went dark.

Chapter Twelve

Rotten food. That's what it was. The stench almost took my breath away. My lungs coughed in protest. I moved a little and opened my eyes, but everything around me was pitch dark. I finally realized that I was inside a huge plastic trash bag, tied securely. My shirt was soaked through with sweat and it was hard to breathe. As I started to thrash about, tearing away at the bag to get out, I felt pain everywhere—especially my head and arm. Then, I was startled by what turned out to be a garbage truck, slam into the trash dumpster I was in.

"Here's one more!" yelled a guy as he tossed a bag into the dumpster. It crashed right on top of me.

I yelled, "Help! Let me out!" as loud as I could, hoping someone could hear me, but my call was drowned out by the sound of the large truck revving its engine. I realized I was about to be part of the morning pickup by the city sanitation department and deposited into the back of a garbage truck. I scrambled the best I could to get out, but since neighboring trash bags weren't solid enough, I couldn't get any traction. It was then that I felt the arms of the trash truck connect with the dumpster and slowly begin its ascent up, up, up, which would eventually send me tumbling over the truck cab and into the back with the rest of the day's collection. I fervently prayed to Jesus to save me from getting dumped, with part two of the prayer being that if I was deposited with the other trash, I would land on something soft. With my luck, this would be his first pickup of the day.

As the container started to lift, I finally tore a small hole in the bag and ripped it open. My right hand reached a side door in the dumpster, which slid open with a metal-to-metal screech as I yanked it. When it was about halfway open, I saw Cassie's neighbor, Michael, standing there with a wide-eyed look of disbelief. I yelled "Help!" again as loud as I could.

Michael ran to the driver's side of the truck, yelling, "STOP! STOP! We've got a dumpster diver! STOP!!"

My arm was flailing out the side door to get the driver's attention when I felt the container's upward motion stop just as it was about to tilt back. The driver reversed the engines, lowered my stinking ride, and landed it on the ground with a loud THUMP that jarred every bone in my body. I sat quietly, glad that my ordeal was over, and thanked Jesus for answering part one of my prayer.

Michael was the first to get to me. "Business must be bad for you to be rummagin' through our trash, PI man," he said. "Grab my hand. Let's get your butt outta there."

Between his brute strength and what little of my own I could muster, I shimmied out of the container and finally stood on terra firma with Michael supporting most of my weight.

"You okay, dude? That's a whopper of a goose egg on your forehead there. Do I need to call an ambulance?"

The garbage truck driver raced over and pretty much repeated the same things that Michael said. I felt not-so-great, but was alive and aware of what was going on, and definitely didn't want an ambulance. I couldn't wait—no, actually I could wait— to see what my forehead looked like.

"I'm okay," I told them. "Nothin' that a nice hot bath and a bucket of ibuprofen won't fix, but thanks anyway. Thank goodness you came out here when you did Michael, or the story of my death might have been on the front page of the paper and obituaries on the same day."

I thanked Michael once again, brushed off some garbage clinging to my clothes and headed for the car.

After a stinky ride home with all the windows down, I went to the laundry room and stripped off my clothes, put them in the washer with detergent filled to the max level, threw a dash of Oxy-Clean in for good measure and set the machine on heavy duty cycle with hot water. I wondered if my blue-striped L.L. Bean shirt would ever be the same. I hotfooted it to the shower and turned up the tap a little warmer than usual. It didn't take long to feel the relief from the water cascading over me and washing away the sweat and that awful garbage smell. Not until I turned to face the oncoming stream of water did I remember the injury to my head. The force and temperature of the water made it sting like hell till I moved my head out of the flow of water. After toweling off and putting on clean clothes, I felt like a million dollars. Well, maybe a half a million, but being clean again was one nice feeling.

After settling down, I thought about the last few hours, second-guessing myself. If I hadn't climbed on that truck, maybe I'd have done something different that would help me figure out who the guy was with Cassie.

But then again, maybe it wasn't a waste of time after all. Surely the truck owner had something important in his truck to do what he did to me for peeping in. I didn't see anything, but he didn't know that. Did he intend to kill me or put me in a situation where I might be killed? Which begged the question: What kind of guy was Cassie hanging around with, anyway?

Was he in on her little secret about her uncle? Did she know what he did to me? And if she did, how could I give Josef Kubrick a good report about her?

Monday morning, I made a point to arrive at work a little later than usual, aware that Michelle would see my wound and worry. With her recent visit to the ER and my injuries from an encounter with a raging idiot, this investigation of Cassie had proven more dangerous for both of us than I first thought it would be.

I climbed up the stairs quietly and opened my office door to be greeted by the smell of stale air trapped inside for the weekend. Our cheapskate building manager always jacked up the offices' temperatures to eighty degrees on summer weekends, and with the hot, humid weather we'd been having, it took at least an hour for the office to cool down on Monday mornings.

As soon as I dropped my computer case and lunch bag on the desk, I heard a gentle knock on the door and a pleasant voice say, "Good morning, Max. Interested in something sweet?"

Chapter Thirteen

I turned and smiled at Michelle, who was standing in the doorway as my heart went pitter-patter from her suggestion. Then I noticed a paper sack from The Happy Bean and Bagel in her hands, and snapped back into reality.

"Sure would, Michelle."

"How about a bear claw and some cinnamon coffee and *goodness gracious what happened to your head!!??*" she nearly shouted.

"I guess the ball cap didn't hide the goose egg, huh?"

"No! It looks like you're starting to turn into part unicorn or mountain goat or something! What on earth happened to you?"

She gently removed my cap and touched near the wound. Then she kissed the tip of her right index finger and gently touched my forehead.

"Thanks, Michelle. It's better already. You see, I was at Cassie's place checking out a truck she had ridden in when I ran into a truck door, but I had a little help. I had just grabbed the door handle so I could look inside when this guy, probably the owner, came by and didn't appreciate my inquisitiveness. After smashing my head, he—or somebody—stuffed me in a big, heavy-duty trash bag and deposited me in a dumpster. At the last minute, I got pulled out by a tenant at Cassie's apartment building, narrowly missing being tossed into the back of a garbage truck. Other than that, and spendin' Friday night with a friend in the ER, it was a pretty quiet weekend." I took a bite of the bear claw and washed it down with a sip of coffee.

"Wait, what? Whose truck was it and what were you looking for? And Cassie rode in it, right?"

"Yes. The owner was someone who knew Cassie. He helped her take down her booth at the race in the park this weekend, drove her to the Porsche dealership, and then back to her apartment. I thought there might be some kind of clue inside the truck that would help me figure out who he was and what he was doing with Cassie."

"Cassie mentioned to me the other day that her cousin Gabriel was coming to visit this weekend and help her with a company event. Must have been him. So did you learn anything?"

"Yep. I learned not to climb onto someone's truck unless it's absolutely necessary."

"Besides that, Max. And what's with the visit to the Porsche dealership?"

"I figure that Cassie might have told cousin Gabriel about her rich uncle's illness, how she is going to be rollin' in the dough soon, and is making plans for how she's going to spend it. But that's just a guess."

"Maybe, but that doesn't sound like Cassie. She seems like a simpler person, not really someone who's into sports cars. When I was at her apartment, she had a Nature Conservancy magazine on her coffee table, and I noticed bills from The National Wildlife Fund and Friends of Radnor Lake on the kitchen table. Her apartment only had basic furniture and decor with nothing fancy. I can't imagine her wanting an expensive gas guzzler like a Porsche."

"Did you see anything else on the table that caught your eye?" I asked.

"Ah, um, nothing else I can think of."

Hm. Either Michelle was hazy on the details after her experience or she was hesitant to talk about something else she saw.

"So back to your story," she said. "This Gabriel guy who may have put you in a trash bag in the dumpster? Didn't that hurt?"

"Since I didn't remember it happening, I don't know. But now, I feel like the loser in a WWE Smackdown event."

"I didn't know this private-eye work could be so dangerous." Michelle said. "How'd you get into this profession, anyway?"

"I first got interested when I was a kid. I had an uncanny knack for finding things. My mom sometimes called me "Max the Hunter" because whenever something was missing or lost, I found it more often than not. Dad called me "Eagle Eye." I also liked to solve puzzles, find hidden objects in pictures in kids' magazines, and make cryptic notes where one letter stands for another and you have to solve it. That was especially handy in writing notes to my girlfriend in the seventh grade in case they were intercepted by someone. Eventually, that all translated to a degree in criminal justice and an apprenticeship with a seasoned PI in town. And then I hung out my own shingle. And what did all that get me? Among other things, a head thumping assault and a ride in a trash dumpster while stuffed in a garbage bag! Ouch!" I grabbed my head and leaned forward from a sudden stabbing sensation of pain.

Michelle gently placed her arm on my shoulder for a light hug and said, "There, there. You'll be okay, Max. Aren't you going to press charges or at least file a police report?"

"If I did that, Michelle, it would blow my cover for sure. First of all, I don't know who to blame unless I ask Cassie. I can't go up to her place and say, 'Hey, Cassie, I was following you and your cousin back from the race on Saturday, looked in his truck while it was parked out back and then he almost killed me and left me for dead in a garbage container. Would you mind giving me his name and address so I can put it on a police report?' I really don't think that will get me anywhere."

"You're right, Max," she said and sighed. "But what are you going to do?"

Before I could answer, my phone started ringing. Sergeant O'Hara's name popped up on the caller ID.

"Hey, O'Hara. What's up?"

"Hi, Jackson. I'm sitting here looking at the coroner's report on the dead Maserati driver. Seems he's here on a work visa, has papers and everything, from Laos, by way of Vietnam, Los Angeles and Iowa City. He's had a number of odd jobs and a clean record except for a car wreck last year in a car that wasn't his. Odds are, he stole the Maserati, too. We're trying to reach family, but that may take a while."

"What about the guy who delivered the package to my office?"

"Not much there either, Max," he said. "I did get to talk to the Kubrick guy in Atlanta, though. He said his secretary hired a delivery firm in Atlanta to deliver the package, who then subbed the job out to another company that delivered to states adjacent to Georgia. The second company didn't have anyone coming to Nashville soon so they hired some guy at a work-pool site and told him what to do. Since it was a cash deal, they didn't have any record of the guy's name or phone number. By the way, Max, we found the owner of the car. The guy lives in Dunwoody and he is none too happy to hear about the damage to his Italian wheels."

"Yeah, telephone pole pieces in the engine compartment and blood stains on the seats and carpet don't do a lot for resale value. So the guy who delivered the package to me was hanging out at a day-workers-for hire location and was paid to deliver the package. Then he stole a Maserati in Atlanta and drove to Nashville. He made the delivery with threats for me not to follow or look for him, which makes sense, since he was driving a stolen car. What I'd like to know is what happened to him, and how did the Asian guy get the stolen car? Maybe my delivery guy stopped at McDonald's and his stolen car got stolen again. It looks like a complicated situation without a whole lot of good clues to go on. Right, O'Hara?"

"Yep. We've got other investigations to work on, and I don't think additional manpower on this case is going to do any good. I'm still worried about who the shooter was and if there was a motive, but unless we uncover more information, I'm at a dead end," the sergeant said. "The bullets came from a rifle. We just don't have any idea who shot it."

Before I could say anything, my phone started vibrating with another call.

"O'Hara," I said, "I'm getting a call from that lawyer in Atlanta. I guess I'd better let you go and see what's up with him. Good luck!"

I hung up quickly and answered the second call before it went to voicemail.

"Well, if it isn't Josef Kubrick. I was just about to call you with an update on my investigation."

"It's about time, Jackson," he said. "But while you're taking your time doing what you're being paid good money to do, I thought I'd tell you what's going on in the Hamilton County Jail. Cassie's cousin, Gabriel Farasinni, is in a heap of trouble.

After the second call interrupted our conversation, Michelle pointed to herself, then held up her right hand with fingers moving like a person walking, pointed toward her office and waved—all the while mouthing words, the only ones of which I understood were walk, office and bye. I interpreted that to mean she had better things to do than stand around listening to me talk on the phone and needed to get back to her work. I nodded, pointed to myself, made the on-the-phone sign with outstretched thumb and pinky on my free hand, and waved back. She covered her mouth stifling a laugh as she walked out the door, her red dress swishing as she turned down the hallway.

"I've got something for you, Josef, but it's not much. First tell me what's goin' on with Gabriel?"

I didn't appreciate his comment about me taking my time, but I figured that hearing about my assailant Gabriel, was more important than my report. Besides, he was one of the candidates in the inheritance competition, and whatever he was up to ultimately affected the object of my investigation, Cassie.

"I got a Google Alert on Gabriel Farasinni this morning. His name came up on a police report. I called a friend in the Tennessee Highway Patrol office in Chattanooga to get some details," Kubrick said. "It turns out that Gabriel Farasinni was caught speeding on I-24 coming down Monteagle Mountain yesterday afternoon. He ignored the cops trying to stop him and led them on a wild goose chase that finally ended just outside Chattanooga near Nickajack Lake. The highway was wet from a thunderstorm and when his truck hit some pooled water on the road, it hydroplaned, slid into a guard rail and got stuck in the mud in the median. He got out of the truck with his hands in the air knowing he was done, and they took him in. The cops found bits of marijuana in the back seat, but not enough to press charges. He already had enough other problems to keep him in jail overnight—in fact, he's still there. The complication is that a blood test revealed the presence of an opioid substance in trace amounts. He didn't admit to using narcotics, but it was in his blood despite his story to the contrary."

"What an idiot, Josef! Cassie doesn't seem to be anything like him. But drugs, evading arrest? Sounds like he's got a problem," I said.

"You've heard of the fruit not falling far from the tree? Gabriel's in a whole different tree from Cassie. Maybe from a different orchard!" replied Josef.

He paused for a moment to collect his thoughts. Or to let me think about his last statement.

"When we started this investigation, Max, I wanted you to have an open mind about the family, so I didn't tell you that this step-cousin Gabriel, who's a little older than Cassie, has never quite been able to find himself, if you know what I mean. He works enough to make ends meet, but loses interest in whatever he's doing after a few months and changes jobs. He's never been fired, but he just doesn't seem to want to punch that clock every day. Work seems to get in the way of fishing, which he does often. Among other things, Gabriel's been a plumber, an electrician, a construction worker, even a WWE fighter for a couple of years. You get the idea. He's had a few brushes with the law, mainly involving fights at local taverns. Kind of has a mean streak. This Gabriel's no angel, Max."

"Ha! A WWE fighter? That explains an unfortunate encounter I had with him this weekend. So tell me, what's next for Gabriel?" I asked.

"I don't know. The DA is working on the case, and he said he'd be in jail for a few days at least till they figure out what to do with him," answered Kubrick.

"Makes sense. I bet the highway patrol didn't care for him racing away like that, putting himself and a whole lot of others in danger. A friend once told me that you better pull over when you see the blue lights because you can't out-run radio."

"Good point, Max. What's this about your unfortunate encounter with Gabriel?" Kubrick asked.

"It's a long story, Josef, but let's just say he didn't appreciate me looking in his truck."

"Okay, So, what have you found out about Cassie?"

"I'm getting mixed signals about her, Josef. On the one hand, she seems like a normal woman her age, working hard, taking care of herself, seeing friends, etcetera. On the other, she spent the weekend with ne'er-do-well cousin Gabriel. She also has a somewhat secret communication with her unapproved Atlanta boyfriend, who tipped her off about her uncle's health condition."

"So she's hanging out with this suspicious character Gabriel and knows about Uncle Claude's diagnosis! That's a cause of concern for me, Max. How'd you find out that she knew about her uncle?"

"I've got a friend, Michelle, who's befriended Cassie and actually read part of a letter written by the boyfriend stating the fact of Claude's condition. Now whether she does something about it or knows or even cares about the inheritance is a whole other thing. What gets me suspicious is that she and Gabriel were shopping at the Porsche dealership on Saturday. Reckon they might be making a deal to split the money if either gets it and then go buy some nice wheels?"

"Who knows, Max. But with Gabriel's recent tussle with the law, I can safely say Claude won't let that young man have a dime of his money. He's out of the running. If your report on Cassie is on the bad side, that will make my job much simpler; letters will be sent to the symphony and botanical gardens detailing generous contributions, and my work will be done."

"Hold on, Josef. I didn't say my investigation was complete. My associate seems to think Cassie's okay, and I trust Michelle's judgement. Hopefully, something will happen this week and I'll get a better idea where Cassie stands. Till then, I better let you go before you start deducting this phone call as an expense against my fee."

"Forget it, Max. Just keep looking and let me know anything else you find out. Oh! By the way, you might be interested to know that Claude Deere is hosting a big party before the Georgia football game this weekend. The invitation says to wear your SEC school colors of choice, as long as they're Arch black and Georgia Bulldog red. He's a huge fan of the silver britches. That's just an excuse for the party, although most invitees won't know the real reason he's throwing it. Have a good day, Max."

I hung up and wondered how in the heck was I going to find anything else about Cassie without either Michelle or me getting closer to her. I didn't want to blow my cover and didn't want to put Michelle—or myself—at risk. Well, too much risk, anyway.

I thought Michelle might want to know what I heard from Kubrick so I walked over to her office. Just as I got to the door, I heard her wrap up a conversation she was having with someone on the phone.

"Oh, thank you, Mr. Tomlin! I can't thank you enough. I'll get back to you tomorrow with my ideas and we'll plan on being there Wednesday night. Thank you so much!" she said, so excited that she jumped up and down, made a couple of spins while smiling and pumping her clenched fists in the air. Then she saw me.

Her cheeks turned red, and she ran over and gave me a bear hug, still grinning from ear to ear.

"What's up with you? You act like you just won the lottery. But wait, you've already done that. Let me guess. You got an invitation to a royal wedding? Got your student loans paid off? I give. What's up?" I asked.

She pointed to the couch and said, "Sit down Max, you won't believe what just happened. I got the most incredible phone call. I just heard back from Mr. Tomlin, a man with whom I've been corresponding for a year. He lives in this old mansion on a farm in rural Williamson County. There have been stories about ghosts in the home, but no one has ever been allowed to research or write about the place. He's getting ready to move and knowing my interest in haunted houses, asked if I'd like to check it out! He wants to have a party at the house for me and some friends and he'll pay for everything! I jumped at the idea and suggested that we have a nice dinner and play a murder mystery game. And I'll get a chance to write about this haunted house including interviews with the current owners and have the experience of staying there overnight. Magazines all over the country will be fighting each other for my inside story about this place. And our party will be just the event to make the article even more interesting. Won't that be great?"

Chapter Fourteen

"That sounds like a real scoop for you, Michelle. Congratulations! But dinner and a murder mystery party? In an old house rumored to be haunted? That seems kind of odd and eerie."

Michelle gave me a funny look.

I quickly added, "But it sounds like a real opportunity too, Michelle," trying not to throw cold water on her excitement.

"Thanks, Max. Even writers like me know there's usually an explanation for strange happenings in a haunted house. Sometimes not. But the problem is that *this party is the day after tomorrow! Wednesday night!* Oh my gosh there's so much to do and it's only two sleeps away!"

"Two sleeps?" I asked.

"Yes. Two sleeps; tonight and tomorrow night. When I was a little girl and didn't understand about days and how to tell time very well—like if my birthday was two days away—my mom would say it was 'two sleeps away' and I knew just what she meant. Two sleeps meant two more nights in bed in my pajamas staring at my Moaning Myrtle poster on the wall before I went to sleep. Then the next morning would be my birthday!"

"Where do moms come up with that stuff?" I said, actually admiring her mother's clever teaching. "But a Moaning Myrtle poster in your bedroom? I always thought she was kind of creepy. Seems like that'd give you nightmares. Anyway, what are you thinking about for the party?"

Michelle looked up in the air at nothing in particular with her hands moving almost as though she was directing an orchestra as she spoke.

"I'm thinking fancy, catered dinner with a string quartet playing while we eat, guests in cocktail attire, and oh, what I'd give for a summer thunderstorm and the power to go out!" she said as she laced her fingers together and held her hands close to her chest as though she was praying.

I looked at her, a bit astonished about these grandiose plans, and wondered how she could pull this off in just a couple of days. Among the things I saw that she couldn't control— besides uninvited guests, like ghosts—was the weather. Although a glance at the weather app on my phone showed she might get her wish for thunderstorms.

"This says we've got a seventy-five percent chance of showers on Wednesday and Thursday, so you may be in luck weather-wise. I'm just not sure how you get the rest done in less than two days."

Michelle snuggled up to me on the couch and said, "With a little help from a friend, I might just make it happen." She fluttered her eyes at me.

I could get used to being this close to her. We'd been within kissing distance twice in the last few minutes. (But who's counting.) I put my arm around her and we snuggled. "Okay. You twisted my arm. How can I help?" I asked.

With a "Thanks, Max!" and a quick peck on the cheek, Michelle catapulted off the couch and walked briskly to her desk. She pulled out the red journal from her top desk drawer and started making notes as she talked and walked back to me.

"I have this friend who has an old roommate who used to work for a guy whose wife is in the catering business. I remember hearing that catering people were usually booked on weekends, but weekdays weren't so busy, so I bet she can provide the food. Decorations, let's see. Hmmmm. I think I want the house to be just the way it is—however that is. I've never actually been there. So that's easy. I bet the Tomlins have some tableware we can use. Music. Max, do you know anyone in the music department at Belmont, Lipscomb or Vanderbilt?"

"A neighbor of mine teaches at Belmont," I answered. "I'll see if she can give me a contact there. So that takes care of date, time, place, food, decor and music. What about the guests? Two days is pretty short notice to invite most anyone to a party."

"Max. I've got friends who would die to come to this party," she said with a giggle. "No pun intended. I'll make the calls now and ask them to bring their spouse or a friend if they want to. Hey, I could ask Cassie! Kill two birds, you know? It'd be interesting to see who she'd bring," she said as she cocked her head and stared toward the ceiling.

"That's not the worst idea. And hopefully whoever she brings has better manners than the last guy I saw with her."

I stood up and walked to the door.

"I'll go make that call, Michelle."

I almost made it to the door when I remembered something important.

"Say! How much does this gig pay?"

"Two hundred apiece. That oughta make it worth their while," she said confidently.

"I'd say it will. Not a bad night's work for a college student. Maybe I should ask them to work up *The Addams Family* theme song and the one from *Friday the Thirteenth.*"

"Oh, Max! Don't be silly! Tell them classical music only. By the way, do you have something appropriate to wear to the party?" Michelle inquired.

"Maybe. Who's my date?" I asked.

"You're going with me," she said with authority.

"Well thanks for the invitation. I'm looking forward to it."

"I can just imagine you now," she said, "in your freshly pressed white shirt and tie, mingling with the crowd, and entertaining everyone with your clever wit and charm."

"Whatever cleverness I have probably won't last long, Michelle. So I'll have to rely on the charm, and that's gonna be a stretch, too," I said. I wondered if going to this party would be something I'd soon regret. But it might just give me an opportunity to find out more about Cassie, and just as importantly, spend more time with Michelle.

"Don't put yourself down, Max. You'll be fine! Now run off and make that phone call!"

Michelle's phone rang as I was about to step out the door. She looked at the phone and gave a big disgusted sigh, so I decided to hang around for a minute.

"Evan! I've told you not to call me ever again! I'm going to hang up and block your calls. *BYE!*"

Michelle turned and looked surprised that I was still there.

She put on her nice smile and said, "Sorry about that, Max. That was just someone I went out with a couple of times that I don't want to hear from again. He's good at pestering me."

While she spoke, she touched her phone several times, likely blocking the caller, deleting the contact, getting him out of her electronic life. Just like that. I figured I didn't have to worry about that Evan guy anymore.

"There, that's done," she said and looked back at me. "Don't you have somewhere to go and make a call?"

"Right! Here I am, walking back to my office to call my Belmont friend," I said as I made a hasty retreat.

The next morning, Michelle and I drove to the Tomlin home, which was about forty-five minutes away. When the GPS told us we had arrived, we spotted the home set back off the main highway with rolling hills in the distance. A gravel driveway leading to the home was lined with huge, century-old oaks that framed the home as we approached it. A four-board white fence on the far side of the oaks separated the driveway from the pasture, where several curious Hereford cows chewed grass and watched us pass by.

I stopped the car in a place to the left and front of the house. Michelle rolled down her window, studied the home and said, "It's perfect, Max! Just perfect!"

The Tomlin home was two stories high, with white clapboard sides and black shutters beside the windows held in place with large iron shutter dogs on either side of every window. A big porch with a light blue ceiling spanned the front of the home. Neat plantings of perennials were spaced intermittently beneath each set of lower level windows. Fresh mulch had been added recently, which made the grounds look very tidy and gave off that new mulch smell. On the second story over the front entrance, two large glass-paneled doors led to a widow's walk, where a pair rocking chairs moved ever so slightly despite the fact that there wasn't much of a breeze as far as I could tell. Knowing the rumors about this house, a little chill went up my spine as I observed their motion.

Gideon and Lucille met us at the door and then gave us a tour of the home. As the morning went on, we all talked as plans for the party started to come together. Musicians had been booked, the caterer was on board, and the Tomlins were making preparations around the big home for guests. Except for being one salad fork short for the table setting and the fact that the house didn't have Wi-Fi, we didn't foresee any real problems.

Throughout the day, I couldn't help but be impressed with Michelle's ability to work under pressure. She didn't seem the least bit frazzled as she confidently checked details off her list. Every few hours, I anxiously eyed the weather app for the following night's forecast only to find that the percentage chance for summer storms intensified with each update.

By that afternoon, all of Michelle's invitees confirmed that they were coming with a date, a friend or solo, and everyone was excited about the party. She wrote each person's name on the guest list, along with something about them for me so I'd be an educated host. A look at the page revealed another writer friend of hers, Natalie Young, and Thomas Wagoneer, a paranormal investigator who was particularly interested in the Tomlin home. Unfortunately for him, the hosts weren't going to allow any equipment to monitor for the presence of spirits. All anyone would be permitted to bring was a basic camera or phone, which the Tomlins said would have to do.

Another invitee was Roberto Grissom, a restoration contractor who specialized in revitalizing old homes. He was interested in how this old mansion was constructed and hoped to get some ideas for his work.

Last on the list was Cassie Simpshire. I was surprised that Cassie would accept the invitation after their last encounter at her apartment. I guess Michelle felt close enough to Cassie to invite her, and Cassie was willing to forgive Michelle for the mail-reading indiscretion. For Cassie to want to attend an overnight party at a haunted house, invited by someone she hadn't known that long, and then stay there with a bunch of total strangers, well, that showed that she either had an adventurous spirit or not much sense. Or perhaps she didn't have anything better to do on a Wednesday night.

Around noon, we all met in the den to wrap things up..

"Gideon and Lucille, I can't thank you enough for allowing us to have this little get-together tomorrow night! My friends and I are all so excited about having a party at a 'haunted' house," she said, making air quotes when she said the word haunted. "All the guests have R.S.V.P.'d, and I believe everything is planned. The caterers will arrive around two tomorrow afternoon, musicians around four, and guests around five-thirty. Max and I will be here at noon to take care of any last minute details."

She added, "Is there anything else I need to do or know about?"

Gideon Tomlin said, "It sounds like you've covered all the bases. You know, we ain't had a party like this in years around here. Heck, havin' all you young folks around tomorrow night will be great fun! And maybe you'll get a good story out of it for your readers, although I doubt it."

"We'll see," Michelle said cheerfully, but I wondered how she'd be a party host and gather information for her story at the same time.

"Okay then, Max and I are on our way out. See you tomorrow afternoon!" she said, grabbing my arm and waving to the couple as we walked out the door.

When we got in the car, I asked Michelle something that had been bugging me ever since I first heard about this party at the haunted house.

"So Michelle, why do these folks want to spend several grand on a party for a bunch of strangers? What's in it for them? Or are they just being nice to you?"

"Here's the deal, Max. I've talked to Gideon Tomlin on several occasions trying to get a story, so we're sort of friends. He knows me, and he evidently trusts me, too. As you can see, the Tomlins are getting up in years, and the other day he told me that they were ready to sell the place and move. The rumor of their house being haunted isn't exactly a positive sales point for realtors and he wants to do something to prove it isn't so that they can get top dollar for the home and property," she answered.

"So that's his angle. However, wouldn't it be best for you if the house *really is haunted*? Say sometime late tomorrow night, the ghost of ole Great Grandaddy Tomlin, killed in the Civil War's Battle of Franklin, bursts through the attic door, races down the stairwell with sabre drawn and scares the hell out of everybody," I said, laughing.

"That would make one heck of a story! Seriously, though. You're right that it wouldn't help resale value, but he claims the house isn't really haunted, despite the rumors. And Gideon is clearly betting on the idea that nothing haunted will happen, my story will end up highlighting his house in a flattering way, and it will help him sell it in the end. Right? Either way, I hope it's a fun party!"

I dropped Michelle off at her place and headed home. When I arrived, I went to the screened-in porch at the back of the house. The sun was beginning to set behind the towering oak trees nearby. I thought about sunrise tomorrow and got a little restless about what the day might bring. Potential storms, food from caterers we've never sampled, college musicians I've never heard, a haunted house, a guest list on which I only knew one person—and that person just happened to be the subject of my investigation!

"Whatcha' so worried about, pal?" bellowed a voice from next door interrupting me from my thoughts.

"You look like you've got a lot on your mind. Detective business gettin' too rough for you?" Colonel Canyon snickered.

"Naw, Colonel. A friend's having a party on really short notice and I'm helping out. Lots of things have to come together for it to be a success."

"So you're helpin'? No wonder you look concerned," he said. "What in the hell does a gumshoe like you know about puttin' on a party?"

"Not much, but thank goodness the party planner seems to have it all together," I answered.

"Wouldn't happen to be that gal you went to lunch with the other day, would it? The one that had you steppin' like a spring pup?"

"Correctamundo, Colonel Canyon. She's a real doll and pretty energetic I must say. She's one reason I want things to go just right. Well, it's good seeing ya. I think I'll turn in for the night."

He gave me a "harrumph" and waved me off as I went back in the house.

Later on, I rested on my bed and stared at the curtains gently stirred by the AC vent, their shadows dancing on a nearby wall illuminated by street lights. I pondered what ghostly things we might experience tomorrow night. *Probably nothing,* I thought. I determined the whole idea of ghosts was just a bunch of malarkey; fun for people who got a thrill out of being scared, and profitable for ghost-tour tour-guides, ready to make fast bucks on gullible tourists. Yep. That's all it was. A bunch of hooey.

I also stared at a painting on my bedroom wall of the Bud Ogles cabin in Gatlinburg, much more relaxing than a poster of Moaning Myrtle. That would give me nightmares. With that, I rolled over, away from the dancing shadows, and drifted off.

Chapter Fifteen

A brisk wind and threatening skies welcomed me as I arrived at the Tomlins' home the next day. Tree branches swayed mightily in the westerly wind as a few leaves blew off the huge oak trees that shaded the front yard near where I parked. Michelle ran out of the house and greeted me with an enthusiastic hug. I could see how excited she was by the look in her eyes. This party was a big deal for her.

"Max! You won't believe how nice the house looks! The Tomlins set the dining room table with some fine old china and more glassware and silver than I've ever seen! It looks like how I imagine Thanksgiving at the Biltmore would be! There's a bouquet of flowers grown right here on the farm in each of the rooms. It's just perfect!"

"That's cool, Michelle, but I thought this was supposed to be a setting for a murder mystery party," I said, wondering if things were going to look a bit too cheery for the occasion.

"It is, and guess what? Mrs. Tomlin loves to decorate the home for Halloween, and even though Halloween is, like, two months away, she brought out the skeletons, witches, ghosts, skulls, candles, and anything that would enhance the haunted house look and scattered them about the home. Our guests are going to love it!"

I thought to myself: *Bouquets of cheerful flowers and Halloween decor. What a combination!*

As the afternoon progressed, caterers arrived with box after box of food to prepare and made themselves at home in the kitchen. Later on, musicians unloaded their instruments and music stands and set up in a corner of the den. By five o'clock, all the servers were dressed in white shirts or blouses with black pants. The quartet looked spiffy too as they tuned their instruments in their white formal shirts with black vests and black pants. The table was dressed elegantly, the food smelled wonderful, and the only damper on the party was that it was raining like hell outside as yet another pop-up thunderstorm came through. Since there wasn't an awning or covered entry, there was no way for guests to avoid the rain as they made their way to the front door.

At five-thirty, Michelle joined me at the front door along with the Tomlins to greet our guests.

First to arrive was Michelle's writer friend Natalie, an attractive, olive-skinned, slight woman with long black hair and dark eyes seated behind oversized red glasses. She wore a stylish short black dress complete with a pearl necklace and crazy-high heels. In addition to carrying a small overnight bag and an umbrella, her escort had to balance her each step of the way across the gravel parking area so she wouldn't fall as they approached the house.

After a big hug, Michelle turned and introduced me to Natalie as "the guy she told her about" which prompted an "Oh!" from Natalie and a full body scan from my wind blown hair to semi-polished shoes.

"Oh!" I responded as I shook her hand and smiled through it all.

The next arrival was Thomas Wagoneer and his date. Thomas was in his early thirties, sported a full brown beard and was dressed like his clothes hadn't seen an iron in years, if ever. As he shook my hand, he didn't look at me, but checked out the interior of the house like he was searching for ghostly hiding places or something. His date, lost in the introductions and his interest in the home, seemed ambivalent about the event and asked me where she could go smoke as she dropped her suitcase in the doorway.

A late-model Range Rover with a black matte finish skidded to a stop in the drive right next to the house, closer than all the other cars. A tall gentleman in a long Filson raincoat walked briskly around the car, opened the passenger door and held out an umbrella for his passenger. She paused to check her hair in the car's vanity mirror before exiting the car, and picked up a small traveling bag. In fewer steps than everyone else took, they were inside.

The driver turned out to be Roberto Grissom. Even more intriguing than his odd car-finish selection, English accent and very proper speech was his lovely date Jessica. When she spoke, I was certain she was from somewhere around Middle Tennessee and that the two of them probably weren't in the same high-school graduating class. She was also a good bit younger than him by at least a decade.

Gideon and Lucille led guests into the den where they gathered around a table covered with several silver platters of hors d'oeuvres. Drinks offered were a variety of red and white wines, a collection of craft beers, sweet tea, and water. Cocktail napkins stamped with a red letter T trimmed in black satin fanned out on the table.

A little before six o'clock, I heard a loud diesel engine roar out front and went to the door to investigate. As I glanced out, I saw a familiar large black truck pull up in the drive. I knew Cassie hadn't arrived yet and figured this had to be her, with cousin Gabriel driving. Of all the people to come to the party— the guy I could thank for the lump that had just about retreated back into my forehead. I thought he was in jail! He must have posted bail and had a reason for coming back to Nashville. Then again, being out on bail, the last thing he needed to do was get arrested again, so, maybe he'd play it cool. *But then I thought, Right! The guy who assaulted me and left me for dead in a dumpster, and resisting arrest from the Tennessee Highway Patrol playing it cool.* Fat chance of that.

The two late-comers rushed to the door and entered more or less soaking wet. Gabriel ran ahead of Cassie and shook like a wet dog when he arrived on the front porch. Large raindrops also pelted Cassie as she ran in, soaking her thin, pale blue blouse which clung to her like a second skin. One hand over her head kept some of the rain off while the other carried a bag, but she still looked like an in-shower, shampoo commercial actress by the time she got to the door.

"Oh, my goodness, Cassie! You're drenched!" Michelle said as she approached from the den. She reached for her soaked friend. "Come with me and we'll get you dried off."

The two of them went down the hallway toward the bathroom, which left me standing with Gabriel.

"Sure looked like rain all day," I said. "Don't you have an umbrella?"

"I did, but the cops confiscated it as evidence in Chattanooga," he answered indignantly.

"What are the cops doing confiscating stuff out of your truck?" I asked.

"That's none of your business really, but if you have to know, I got stopped there a few days ago after some bad luck. Cops took everything out of the truck, including the umbrella, and found some stuff they shouldn't have. Cassie here posted bond for me on the terms that I'd play nice and go with her to a stupid party at a stupid haunted house way out in the boonies with a bunch of idiots I've never met. So far, all I've got out of this party is a soaked jacket. I hope they've got a beer on that refreshment table," Gabriel said as he handed me the jacket and proceeded to the dining room.

I got the feeling Gabriel didn't recognize me. Maybe he was expecting me to be dead, not a greeter at the stupid party at a stupid haunted house way out in the boonies.

I took his extra-large, rain-soaked camo jacket and hung it in the closet. I wondered why he hadn't offered the coat to Cassie when they came in. It would have been more than enough to cover her smallish frame and him as they ran to the house.

After a while, Michelle returned to the den with Cassie, wearing a red blouse in place of the pale blue one and only the ends of her hair showing dampness from the rain.

Michelle continued to the middle of the room, cleared her throat and got the attention of the quartet who played an attention-getting "Ta-da!" so she could offer an official group welcome.

"Hi, everyone! It's nice to see you on this rainy day. Thank you for coming to our murder mystery party! We are so thrilled to welcome you as our guests, and we're especially thankful for our hosts, Gideon and Lucille Tomlin, for opening this space to us." A polite applause was directed toward the Tomlins.

She continued. "We have a fine dinner for you tonight, which will begin shortly, then we'll play our murder mystery game. The object of the game will be to determine who is the murderer. We'll pass out cards giving each of you your roles; one of you will be secretly chosen as the murderer, and another, the victim."

As soon as Michelle said, "victim," the room flashed with light from a monstrous bolt of lightning and then a boom of thunder that rattled our bones. The jolt was followed by a blood-curdling scream that came from the kitchen. Then, all the lights went out and several guests in the room echoed the scream.

And there we were: Michelle got her lights-out, summer thunderstorm wish, the home was filled with screams, and the evening had just begun.

Chapter Sixteen

Storm clouds covered the western sky, and obscured the few remaining rays of sunset from entering the windows. Power was out in the house and only lit candles in the dining room provided light for us to see until several guests activated the flashlight app on their cellphones. I asked Michelle to stay with the guests as Gideon and I hurried to the kitchen to investigate the source of the scream.

John, the catering manager, was at the kitchen sink holding a blood-soaked cloth around the right hand of Marcia, one of the cooks. The small hispanic woman was sobbing as she supported her injured hand over the sink where cold water from the tap bathed the towel over her wound in an effort to stop the bleeding.

"What happened, John?" I asked, hoping she hadn't cut off a finger.

"Marcia was chopping carrots when the lightning struck which made her jump and cut her thumb. She's bleeding like hell. I'm going to have to take her to the ER for stitches and probably a tetanus...."

Another loud CRACK outside the kitchen window interrupted his diagnosis. We looked out the kitchen window and saw a large branch from a tree hit by lightning slowly fall toward the house. Then, everyone ducked as one branch barely poked through the window—right where Marcia and John stood . The main trunk fell to a loud THUNK on the ground outside. Marcia and John jumped back with eyes closed and heads turned away from the window as glass from the shattered window flew through the air and landed on the kitchen counter and floor. He managed to keep a hold of the cloth on her hand.

In the dining room, guests were startled when yet another branch from the tree fell and landed outside the dining room on the roof of an attached screened-in porch. I ran back into the room just in time to watch the branch settle briefly on the roof, then fall, taking the roof with it and landing inside on the porch floor. Old leaves that had collected in the gutters were flushed by pooled rain, down and into the porch. Porch furniture was getting soaked. I almost hesitated to look outside to see if another limb was headed our way.

I turned to Michelle to see how she was holding up during all the excitement. She had a concerned look on her face, but in a moment, forced a smile and turned to me expectantly. *What next?* her expression said.

John came into the dining area with Marcia and said, "We're going to the hospital. I've left Marcel in charge. Don't worry. He's used to running things and will do a great job. Dinner's almost ready, anyway. We had to trash the carrots because of the glass and ah, you know, because of the accident, but everything else was safe in the ovens and refrigerator, thank goodness."

John and Marcia walked briskly to his car for their trip to the hospital. Guests looked around at Michelle, wondering what was going to happen next. She took a deep breath and addressed the crowd. "Wow! That's some start to our party, isn't it? Is everybody okay?"

Everyone nodded a cautious yes. I surveyed the crowd and didn't see anyone too shaken by the events of the last few minutes. Lucille Tomlin disappeared right after the second lightning strike and returned to the room carrying several brass candlesticks, long red tapers and a bunch of matchbooks stored in a Mason jar. Gideon said he'd get something to temporarily seal the kitchen window to keep the rain out.

As Lucille unwrapped the tapers and placed them in the slightly tarnished brass candlesticks, she said, "I don't know how long the power will be out, folks, so I brought these candles for us to use now, and for later, when you go to your rooms. Since we're out here in the country, we're often the last ones to get power back, but if there's only one line down closer to town that affects us, it might be sooner than later. We just never know."

"Thanks for the candles, Lucille," Michelle said. "Maybe they'll get it fixed soon."

Michelle, the eternal optimist.

Another loud boom of thunder right overhead startled us all momentarily and didn't offer much hope that we'd get electricity back anytime soon.

Michelle announced to the crowd a little later that dinner was about to be served. "If everyone would take your seats, we'll get started. The place cards show you where to sit."

Hosts Lucille and Gideon were seated at opposite ends of the big oak farm table, while Michelle and I were opposite each other in the middle. In a clever move, Michelle had placed Cassie to my right and Gabriel on the opposite side and far end away from us.

From the glow of candlelight, Gideon offered thanks, then we started the meal. I was thankful that the kitchen had a gas stove and all the food was cooked and served hot for our guests. I was thankful that Marcia wasn't hurt any worse than it appeared. I was also thankful that despite all the setbacks, Michelle was still enjoying herself.

The quartet started their dinner music after the blessing. It was tastefully played at a volume we could enjoy and still have conversation. The occasional booms from outside didn't necessarily stay in time with the music, but added an interesting percussive touch, I thought.

Servers handed bowls of entrees and sides at several places around the table for us to serve ourselves and pass. A big bowl of homemade mashed potatoes with a yellow dollop of butter slowly melting on the top was the first one to come to me. When finished, I passed the bowl to Cassie.

While serving herself a small scoop, she turned her head and said under her breath, "You'll have to excuse my cousin, Gabriel. He's been in trouble with the law a few times and is a little rough around the edges. But he's really not that bad a guy; just kind of possessive about his stuff—especially his truck."

"Tell me about it," I said as I remembered our encounter. "He may fit right in as the perfect guest for a murder-mystery party," I said. "So why did you bring him?"

A big plate of hot fried chicken came from my left. It was the crispy kind that I never could seem to master frying at home. I helped myself to a piece then passed the plate to Cassie.

"We're cousins, you see, and we needed to talk about family business. There's a lot going on in our family these days and we need to be prepared."

"Just what is it you need to be prepared for?" I questioned her as a steaming bowl of green beans (my favorite) arrived. I couldn't believe I pried with this question, but Cassie seemed to want to talk. And if she wanted to open up, I was ready to listen.

"Well, since you're a friend of Michelle's, I guess I can confide in you. You see, relationships have been strained within our family for a long time, and I think it's time Gabriel and I got a start on getting things sorted out so there's at least a little peace and harmony. We've got one cousin who was caught shoplifting recently in Atlanta. Another cousin, Layla, a surfing instructor and bartender in Florida, attracts the wrong kind of guys. She wears her little bikinis around and has a knack for finding trouble before it finds her. Add those to Gabriel's recent brush with the law, the fact that our parents never really got along, and well, you get the picture," she said, carefully slicing half a spiced pear from the serving dish, draining the juice, and setting it on her plate. "I'm batting a thousand when it comes to loser cousins."

"You don't have to sugarcoat it for me, Cassie. Tell me how you really feel," I said, hoping to break the seriousness a little. "So what makes you think you can straighten things out?"

"Good question, Max. You see, we have this wealthy uncle who's pretty old, like over seventy, and I hear he isn't in good health. Since the people I mentioned are just about all the close family he's got left, we've always assumed he'd leave his wealth to the cousins. But what I'm concerned about is that if the others get a big pile of money, they'll just continue their reckless lifestyles, which will eventually catch up with them and, well, bad things will happen. Kind of like they already have, except more so. I can't decide if I should tell my uncle about them or not. It would be the truth, and he should know, but if I do, it'll make me look like a tattletale to keep them out of his will."

Her words showed good intentions, but made me wonder whether she really did care about these other cousins and her uncle, or if she was just trying to make sure she got the bigger piece of the pie.

"What if he decides to give it all to you, since from what you say, you appear to be the only one that's not in trouble?" I asked her. "Or maybe he would consider giving it to a charity or something?"

"With all my student debt and the store's start-up expenses, I guess it would be nice to get a lot of money, but I don't know how the cousins would take that. As long as they were around, I'd be concerned they might do something rash to get even. When I used to see them on rare family reunions and other visits, they were just horrible—lying, fighting, showin' out - you name it. After each visit, I hoped I'd never have to see them again."

"That sounds like a real mess, Cassie."

"So tonight starts my rehab plan with Gabriel," she said. "If he behaves on this little outing, it might just benefit him in the future. I won't tell my uncle about him, and his good behavior will keep him out of jail. If not, and he keeps running into trouble with the law, he's on his own."

I asked myself if Cassie was showing tough love, determination or ruthlessness? I still wasn't sure quite exactly where Cassie was going. However, it was interesting to get her insight. That is, unless she was feeding me a bunch of lies. Heck, for all I knew, she could have found out that I was hired to investigate her and was trying to make herself look good.

Meantime, despite the earlier events, our guests seemed to have settled down and were enjoying themselves. The dining room's ambience fit the evening perfectly; the place was elegant if dim, with the only light in the room provided by candles and their mirrored reflections. The room was abuzz with several conversations. Gabriel was the lone quiet guy, chowing down like nobody's business on a second helping of potatoes.

Thomas was having an especially good time, having been seated next to Roberto's date. Her name was Jessica, a beautiful blonde wearing a form-fitting red dress that had captured his attention (as it did mine) when she arrived. She had the charm of an actress and the grace of a dancer, and I don't know if that's what had him intrigued or if it was her other attributes. She seemed to enjoy Thomas' conversation since Roberto pretty much ignored her to pepper Gideon with endless questions about the home and how it was constructed.

I looked up and caught Michelle's eye. We locked glances for a time that became a bit uncomfortable, but then she smiled a big smile and leaned over to ask Lucille a question.

Outside, a howling wind blew low notes through the trees as higher pitches whistled through the old windows in the dining room. The wind velocity increased so much that the front door of the house was blown wide open, knocking over a couple of potted schefflera plants in the foyer before Lucille had a chance to get to the door and close it securely. Cassie got up from the table and rushed over to help Lucille set the pots back in their place. Then she found a broom in a closet near the front door and swept up the dirt that had spilled. The Southern boy in me thought, *Her mama raised her right.*

After watching Cassie's quick, unsolicited clean-up, I realized that if Michelle hadn't arranged this party, I wouldn't have seen this side of Cassie or had that conversation with her during dinner. In fact, except for what little I'd found out on my own, most of the best information about Cassie had come from Michelle, one way or another. I began to see that she was an important part of this investigation. And as a bonus, she was adorable, and I certainly enjoyed being with her. I wondered if the feelings were mutual.

Chapter Seventeen

A couple of hours later, the power still hadn't come back on. We'd finished dinner and dessert and had talked enough that those of us who didn't know each other well had just about run out of things to say. Candles did help light up the place, but after a few hours, my eyes were tired of squinting just to see. We tried to play the murder mystery game, which was something most everyone was looking forward to, but since it was pitch dark outside and there weren't that many candles around, we couldn't read our roles very well on the cards that Michelle passed out. And it was almost impossible to see people or furniture as we walked about the room, which caused safety concerns. After a few awkward minutes of trying to play, Michelle announced that we would stop the game and might resume play if the lights came back on. Meanwhile, we just sat around in the den and parlor and visited.

At nine, the musicians finished their last number, packed up and left for the night. The caterers weren't far behind them. Gideon brought out a few bottles of wine fermented from muscadines grown on his farm. It may have saved the later part of the evening since there really wasn't much to do but sit around and talk.

Lucille started showing guests to their rooms around ten. Most rooms in the home were cozy-small with one double bed; some had two twins. I didn't know about everyone's sleeping arrangements, but I figured some guests may have shared a room depending on their situation and some didn't, not that that was any of my business. I just knew that I got the big couch in the parlor, the red one with curved, carved wood armrests and a seat so firm you could bounce a quarter off it. Lucille had left a nice pillow and a sheet though for me to use. I found out later that Michelle wanted me there so I'd be close to the middle of the house in case there were any problems, and also because they'd used all the bedrooms for our guests.

After everyone had settled down, Michelle came down the stairs and sat on the couch with me.

"So, what did you think of the party, Max?" she asked.

"It was a great event, except for the part where the lights went out. Still, I think everyone had a good time. How 'bout you?"

"Same here. I would definitely call it a success! I mean, the food was good, music was perfect, and even though the weather caused some problems, it created the vibe I wanted—dark and mysterious. I was mesmerized by the reflection of candle flames flickering in the mirrors while we were eating dinner. If only we could have played the murder-mystery game. That was going to be fun, but it just didn't work out. Whew! It's been quite an evening and I'm worn out."

"Wait, Michelle. Isn't this the time where some apparition shows up and we find out the real story of the haunted Tomlin mansion?" I asked with a sly grin.

"Mmmm, maybe, but it's not looking so good right now for that to happen," Michelle said. "We've already had intense lightning flashes, booming thunder, tree branches coming through windows and knocking down porches, screams from the kitchen and guests. Surely we've had about all the excitement we're going to have for one night."

"So," she said, slapping her hands to her thighs and smoothing her skirt as she stood up. "I'm going to turn in. If you need me, I'm in the second room on the right at the top of the stairs. The first room is Gabriel's, so don't get them mixed up," she said smiling.

Then Michelle leaned over to me and planted a soft kiss on my lips that lingered. And lingered. Just as I was getting used to it, she pulled away and said softly, "Thanks, Max. You've been more than a friend tonight."

Michelle tiptoed up the dark stairway, stopped at the top to give me a quick wave, then disappeared down the hallway.

I took a deep breath, satisfied with how the evening went, and closed my eyes trying to permanently seal the memory of that kiss in my brain. And was the statement about her room location an invitation or just for my information if I needed her? I guessed since I was more or less on guard duty downstairs, it was for the latter.

I kicked off my shoes, took off my tie, and unbuttoned the top button of my shirt to get comfortable. With power out, the house had become a little stuffy, although the storm had brought cooler air and a breeze coming through the windows that made things bearable without the AC. I placed a pillow at one end of the couch and settled back. I figured it would be a little more comfortable than sleeping on the floor, except for the large metal buttons holding the leather fabric in place that seemed to poke me in all the wrong places.

It was very dark, but my eyes became accustomed to the unlit home to the point that it was possible to make out furniture in the room and where pictures were hanging on the walls. The thought occurred to me that when the power did come back on, the downstairs might be lit up like a shopping mall grand opening. But then pleasant thoughts of Michelle and how she looked at me after the kiss filled my brain, and I snuggled with the pillow and dozed off.

Footfalls startled me from sleep as I looked through foggy eyes to see Jessica coming down the stairs with a small flashlight in hand. I sat up, ran my hand through disheveled hair and tried to figure out if this was a dream or really happening. When she sat down next to me and I got an ever so slight scent of her perfume, I decided I was awake and this *was* happening.

"Hey, Jessica. Is everything okay?"

"I guess that depends on your definition of 'everything,'" she said as she sat next to me, crossed her arms and stared past me looking out the window.

It seemed like we were in a psychiatrist-office moment, except both client and doctor were sitting on the couch. I didn't know if I was supposed to talk, ask a question or let her continue. Besides, her house shoes with heels and Jessica Rabbit pajamas on a leopard print background almost caused me to chuckle.

"Cool pajamas! They're really appropriate with you being named Jessica and all. She wore a red dress in the movie, didn't she? Kind of like you did tonight."

"Well at least somebody's paying attention!" she said.

I began to get some insight as to why she came downstairs.

"All I ask for is a nice romantic night on the town, and what do I get? A party out in the country with a bunch of people I don't know, a scary thunderstorm—I hate storms, Max—a twin-bed bedroom that's decorated with princesses and unicorns, a lovely view of the little family cemetery outside my window, and a boyfriend who hasn't paid one iota of attention to me! And to boot, *she's here!*" Jessica said, exasperated.

"Who's here?" I asked.

"That woman with the long brown hair and hot body," she answered.

I hesitated to ask "Which one?" since I could think of two women here who might fit that description.

" … and the dark brown eyes that hide secrets she doesn't know that I know about!" she continued.

"That would be Cassie," I said, just to make sure we were on the same page.

"Cassie, Schmassie! The one who 'hired' my boyfriend Roberto to help make her store downtown look Nashville-cool with old architectural knick-knacks and crap. Before Cassie moved into the store, she called him almost every day for *two* months so he could inspect things she'd found at salvage places and see if he approved. I wondered if that's all she wanted him to inspect! The one time I went to the store with him, she was wearing leggings and a top so tight it left nothing to your imagination. I mean nothing. She'd stand closer to him than necessary as she spoke, gently touching him when making a point. She always smiled that flirty smile when he spoke. And when she walked away, I swear she had a little extra sway in her hips. I just know that ..."

"Whoa, Jessica," I said trying to calm her down. "Do you have proof that something was going on?" I asked.

"No, but she still hasn't paid for his design services as far as I know. He says she's still getting on her feet in the business and will pay him back when she can."

"I'm sorry about all that, Jessica, and can see why you're upset. But look, it's late. Why don't you just try to forget about it and get some sleep?"

"I guess you're right, Max. Thanks for listening. Sometimes I get carried away. Still, I just don't think this thing with me and Roberto is going to work. He's obviously not that interested in me, and lord knows I've been trying to get him interested."

She paused and said. "You and Michelle seem to be good friends."

"Yep, good friends," I answered. "We work in the same office building and I'm just helping her out tonight."

"Oh, I see," she said as she stood up. I stood up as well as she took a step toward the stairs, and then turned back.

"You know, I have my own interior design business. I'd love to come by your place sometime and give you some ideas," she said with a smile. "At your office or home. Either one."

"Sure! When either place needs a makeover, I'll give you a call."

Jessica grabbed an ink pen from the table, reached for my wrist, and wrote her number inside the palm of my right hand. Then she switched on her flashlight which lit the way up the stairs to her room, climbed the stairs, and then turned left at the top. A door opened and closed, and the house was dark and quiet once more. I glanced at the number on my palm, already blurring from sweat. Then I took a deep breath and settled back to sleep, seeing images of Jessica and Jessica Rabbit in my brain.

Chapter Eighteen

Sometime later in the night, I was startled awake by a "clunk-clunk" sound. I shot up and looked around, trying to determine the source of the noise. Any odd sound in a strange house thought to be haunted, whether it was or not, was sure to get my attention. In the general direction of the den, I spied a red light moving toward me. After a few blinks of my eyes to focus, I saw that the red light was carried by someone moving it left to right and back again.

I stood up and said in a whisper, "Who's there?"

A voice answered, "It's me. Thomas. What are you doing down here?" he answered.

"I was about to ask you the same thing," I responded. "What's with the red light?"

"It's a thermal imaging device attached to my iPhone," he said. "It detects anything that gives off heat. I've found it useful in my line of work. You know, looking for spirits."

"You know you weren't supposed to bring anything like that here," I said.

He continued to sweep the room with the device, looking at the screen as he ignored my protest. "Yeah, well, I've got a lot more sophisticated equipment that I didn't bring and figured that this small device wouldn't matter. I walked the hallways upstairs to see if I could get any hits, but didn't have any luck." Thomas kept walking as he talked, but then stopped suddenly. "Hey! Wait a minute! What's that?"

I walked over to him and looked at the phone screen. His phone started to emit a soft beep as Thomas pointed it toward the front door. A fuzzy red image appeared on the screen. We both looked outside and made out a figure in a white gown walking slowly on the porch, almost zombie-like, and holding a small lantern. Thomas and I both froze, fixed on the subject as it made its way to the corner of the house and out of sight.

We both jumped when we heard someone coming from behind us. Gideon Tomlin was rushing down the stairs carrying a flashlight, his face showing concern.

"Have you seen Lucille, boys?" he asked. "She wasn't in the bed, and I was afraid she's having another one of her spells, as she calls them."

After spotting something on his phone and then being surprised by Gideon, an anxious Thomas said, "I don't know about your wife, but I think we spotted a ghost on your front porch, carrying a lantern and walking around. Max was about to go outside and check on it, weren't you, Max?"

I glanced at Thomas in disbelief: a real live ghost hunter didn't want to investigate the apparition himself? Before I had a chance to speak, Gideon said, "I doubt that's a ghost, fellas. Lucille's been known to sleepwalk after a stressful day, and I'd say this one certainly counts as one. She was wearing a long white gown when she came to bed. Is that what your ghost was wearing?"

Suddenly, the back door behind us opened. We all turned and saw Lucille enter the dining room carrying the same little lantern. She approached us and shook her head in disbelief.

"What are y'all doing up at this time of night! Y'all better get some sleep 'cause that rooster will be crowing pretty soon," she said, then turned to make her way up the stairs.

"Happens every time," said Gideon. "When I see her at night at the end of her walk, she talks to me like I'm the one actin' weird, and then she goes right back to bed. And in the morning, she won't remember a thing, but she'll ask me what the lantern's doing on her nightstand. And just so you'll know, we ain't had a rooster around here since forever!"

"So much for your ghost hunting, Thomas. Good try, though," I said, trying to comfort the obviously disappointed guy.

"I thought I had something," he said. "But that's how it goes. Maybe I'll get lucky next time."

Thomas looked out the front door again and let out a big sigh.

"I'm gonna walk around a few more minutes then get back to bed, he said."

With that, he turned his phone off and opened the front door to go outside.

Chapter Nineteen

*T*he next morning, clouds had cleared. The previous day's storm had not only sucked the moisture out of the air, but left us with slightly cooler temperatures and forecasted highs for the day in the upper eighties. So much for a mild summer day in the South.

Since many of our guests had to go to work the next day, they were all out of the house by eight o'clock. Lucille had prepared warm sausage biscuits wrapped in tin foil and coffee in to-go cups for them to pick up as they left. We said hasty goodbyes as our guests scurried off to their destinations.

Afterwards, Michelle and I enjoyed a light breakfast by ourselves in the kitchen. Gideon was cutting a tree that fell behind the house and Lucille had gone to let out the chickens and gather eggs from the coop.

"What a night!" exclaimed Michelle. "That was so much fun, even though it was a ton of work!"

"You did a great job, Michelle. Everyone had a good time, except maybe for Marcia when she cut her hand. And then there's Gabriel who was forced to come and didn't want to be here in the first place, but figured it was better than a jail cell in Chattanooga. And Jessica told me her boyfriend ignored her the whole time, so she was pretty much bummed the whole night. Except for those things—which were out of our control —it was a good night."

Michelle looked surprised. "You sure picked up on a lot of things," she said. "I guess I was too involved in making sure everything went smoothly to catch those details. Anyway, I did get to visit with some friends I hadn't seen in a while."

Michelle nervously fiddled with her necklace, which had a small gold locket attached. I'd seen her wear it before—in fact she wore it most of the time. The last time I saw her holding it was when we were at the pawn shop as she studied the diamond rings. Maybe it was just a nervous habit.

"Oh, yeah! I hadn't told you that Thomas was snooping through the house last night and thought he'd tracked a ghost walking on the front porch. I was down there when it happened."

"He did!? Tell me more! And why'd he do that? He knew he wasn't supposed to bring any equipment here. Finally, I have something for my story!" she bubbled.

I told her the story about Thomas, his phone, the figure in white, the lantern, the slow Zombie walk, and how we stood inside watching what looked like a ghost.

Michelle's eyes got big as she leaned over and grabbed my wrist.

"What happened next? Did he go outside to investigate?"

"Hardly. Your chicken-ass friend Thomas volunteered me to go while he stayed inside to 'monitor the situation.' As I was headed to the door, Gideon came down the stairs. He heard what we were talking about and said to not get excited because it was only Lucille. He said she would sleep-walk some nights, wandering about the house and sometimes outside on the porch, but never went any farther."

"Well that explains a lot," she said.

"Explains what, Michelle?"

"It explains why a ghost has been seen at the house, Max! With Lucille wearing a white gown and carrying a light, anyone driving down the main highway looking this way with a little imagination might think they saw an apparition walking on the porch. Gideon probably never thought about that, and Lucille was none the wiser. Mystery solved!"

"What's that going to do for your story, lady? Isn't your audience a bunch of weirdos getting their thrills about looking for ghastly stories with blood and guts and creatures from other dimensions scaring the wits out of unsuspecting victims? The way this one turned out, it's just like a false alarm."

"Wait a minute, Buster. My readers are not a bunch of weirdos. They're everyday people with a special interest in the supernatural. Some of them have had their own interaction with spirits and are curious about what others have experienced. When I write this story, I'll build up the mystery of the 'female spirit who walks the porch at night.' After building up numerous sightings over the years, I'll drop the bombshell about it really being the homeowner sleepwalking in her nightgown carrying a lantern. People were fooled all these years, and they'll think it's funny. My readers will love it!"

"Whatever you say, Michelle. I guess I don't understand your line of work very well."

"What's to understand? Besides, yours doesn't make sense to me sometimes either. So I guess we're even."

"Right. Speaking of my work: I had a great conversation with Cassie last night, so the trip wasn't completely a bust for me. You know, one minute she seems like an innocent woman trying to make better for herself and her family, and other times she seems like a schemer trying to place all the good cards on her side and stack the deck with bad ones on others. I also found out from Jessica that she and Cassie have a little history—evidently vying for the same man."

"Hmm," said Michelle. "And I thought she was just interested in that boyfriend in Atlanta!"

Michelle and I gathered our things and headed out to the car. As we walked down the steps, Lucille came around the corner of the house carrying two well-loved woven baskets loaded with brown eggs.

"I was hopin' to catch you two before you left," she said as she placed one basket down on the ground and stood up to wipe her brow.

"Here, Michelle. This one's for you," Lucille said, handing Michelle the gift.

Michelle held out her hands to accept the basket which must have had a couple of dozen eggs inside. She smiled the smile of one who'd just made a new friend.

Michelle picked one up and said, "They're still warm! I can't take all these eggs! And this basket. It must be a family heirloom!"

"Sure you can, besides I don't have anything else to put them in. Just bring it back next time you're in the area. This is just our way of saying thank you for hosting such a fun time last night. We haven't ever done anything like that before! It was so nice to meet you and your friends."

"I appreciate you for offering your place to us and all the work you did to host. I do hope that the storm damage to your house isn't too bad."

About that time, the revs of a chainsaw stopped and we saw Gideon come around the house.

"Glad I caught you before you left! We had a big ole time last night and can't thank you enough for all the work you did. Don't be a stranger, now. Y'all get on your way and I'll get back to cuttin' up that tree."

"Do you want me to stay and lend a hand?" I asked. "I'm not good with the chainsaw, but I can carry stuff for you."

"Mighty nice of you to offer, but Clayton and his boy from down the road are comin' by to help. In fact, they're pullin' in the driveway now," Gideon said as he pointed to an old pickup approaching the home.

We said our goodbyes then loaded up the car. As we drove off, we waved once again to Lucille and traveled down the gravel driveway.

Michelle pointed out the neat little farms along the way back home down the highway that would eventually take us to Lewisburg Pike.

"This part of the county is just beautiful. I've always wondered what it would be like to live in the country. Maybe have some chickens, a few cows, a garden for flowers and one for vegetables, white lace curtains on the windows gently blowing with breeze ..." as her voice trailed off still in the dream.

"Sounds nice. But do you know the first thing about taking care of livestock, or the difference between a weed and a vegetable? And wouldn't you miss reliable cell and internet service, if you could even get those things? You'd be far from town when you ran out of something or wanted to visit people, you'd..."

"Stop it! You're ruining my fantasy, Max!" Michelle interrupted. "I guess all that would be true, but still, it would be more peaceful than living in the city or suburbs."

"I think I could get used to living out here, too. I'd like the clean air, fewer sirens, less traffic, and a less hectic setting in general. All of that would surely make life less stressful," I said. "And when you ever did run out of something, you'd just 'do without,' like my granddad used to say."

"Yeah, there's always a way," she said with a sigh as she played with her locket again.

"I noticed you holding that locket before. Is it special?" I asked, hoping I wasn't being too nosy.

"It's from my mom and dad. They gave it to me on my sixteenth birthday, and I've worn it ever since."

She opened the locket, leaned over and held it out to me where I could see the inside.

"That's a photo of them on the left and me on the right."

"Nice. Do they live around here?" I asked. Michelle hadn't told me about where she grew up or anything about her family.

"No, they live in Asheville, in the same house where I grew up. It was just them and me; no siblings. I did have a few close cousins who lived nearby. We were almost like brothers and sisters since we were always together—went to the same schools, church, you know. Dad was an engineer who wrote technical documents on mountain highway construction and mom was an accountant for several small businesses in the area. They loved to hike and had lots of good places to explore nearby. Mom is a regular 10K runner and even won her age group at a race this year! She's amazing! You'd like her, Max. Our family loved camping and hiking trips to the mountains, but they were in such good shape, sometimes it was all I could do to keep up when I was a kid! How about your family, Max? I don't know anything about them except that you grew up in Nashville."

"We lived out Lebanon Road, east of Nashville. My mom and dad had three kids; I was the youngest. Dad started a building supply business between Nashville and Donelson that was very successful and was eventually bought out by a huge hardware megastore. They always wanted a place on the Gulf coast, so when they sold the business, they bought a house near Destin. It sits right on the beach! There's a small lake beside them where they keep a kayak for rowing. They love it and I love visiting them there. My two older brothers live with their families nearby in Franklin and Mt. Juliet."

"Cool! Do you and your brothers get together very often?"

"Yeah, for holidays and an occasional ball game. They're really pretty busy with work and kids' activities, but we stay in touch. Look, we're almost to your place."

I pulled in the driveway, punched in the code at the gate, drove in and parked the car. We got out, and I carried Michelle's small travel case to the back door.

When we got to the door she unlocked it, opened it slightly, then turned and said, "About last night..."

"Yes?" I answered.

"That goodnight kiss. That was ... very nice. Very nice indeed. When I went to my room, I was blushing beet red. Could you tell?"

"Well, no, 'cause it was dark in the house and you were walking away from me," I answered. "I probably was, too. Did you notice?"

"No, silly. It was dark in the house and I was walking upstairs away from you, smarty pants," she said with a laugh.

Michelle looked down at her feet then back at me, standing almost toe-to-toe with her. So close I could smell her perfume. Or was it shampoo? Or body wash? Maybe it was just Michelle. She continued.

"That kiss. It was so gentle and real; not forceful or overly passionate," she said with a slight blush growing on her cheeks. "When I got to my room, I couldn't help but wonder how you learned to kiss like that."

"If you must know, there was this girl my senior year in high school who …."

"That's quite enough information, Romeo," Michelle interrupted me with a laugh. "It's just that I was hoping for a repeat performance. Do you have some time before you go back home?"

She tilted her head slightly and twisted one long lock of hair, smiled at me, then turned and opened the door the rest of the way, waiting for my answer.

I walked just inside the room, placed my hands on her hips and gave her a quick peck on the cheek.

"I guess that means yes," she said. She closed the door behind me and locked it. "Follow me, handsome."

We took a few steps toward the den, but were startled by a voice coming from near the couch.

"I shore hope I ain't interrupting some intimate romantic rendezvous!" the voice announced.

Chapter Twenty

"**E**van! WHAT ARE YOU DOING HERE!!"
Michelle yelled.

"How did you find me and, and HOW DID YOU GET IN MY HOUSE?" she seethed.

Michelle was livid. I'd never seen her so mad. I figured this was most likely the Evan who called when I was in her office. He was still lying on the couch staring at us with a stupid grin. Unkempt long hair, several days of stubble, untucked cowboy shirt and blue jeans with holes in both knees made him look like yet another bro-country singer. Boots and all. The smell of alcohol and his slurred speech revealed a morning drinking session ... or one heck of an evening. He stood at average height and weight, with a slight pooch in the stomach. Adding his drunken state to the formula, I was convinced that I could take him if need be. The only thing that concerned me was the bone handle, brass pommel hunting knife sheathed in his belt holster.

He stood up and faced us.

"Piece-a-cake, Michelle. You always said you wanted a house in this part of town, so I did me some drivin' and bam! There it was. Right in front of me. Your M&M neon sign glowing in the front window. M&M. Michelle and McCartney. So I just parked my car down the street, found a bathroom window open in back of the house and let my little ole self in. By the way, where's your manners? Ain't ya gonna introduce me to your friend, Romeo somethin' or 'nother?"

Michelle reached for her phone.

"His name is Max and I'm calling the cops, Evan! Get out while you can, or I'm pressing charges."

I slowly moved between Michelle and Evan as he took a step in our direction. He ran his hands through his hair then gave Michelle a thorough ogle and smiled a wicked grin.

We both listened to Michelle talk to the 911 operator. She told them someone had broken into her house and that he was still here. She mentioned her boyfriend was with her and was a witness.

Evan slowly took another step, straightened his back, and said drunkenly, "Boyfriend, huh? I used to have that title, although not for long."

Evan gave me a red-eyed glare and said, "Let me tell you a few things about this little lady before you get all caught up in love. Just because I made friends with a cute little country singer, this here sweet thing threw me out and wouldn't have me back. Can you believe that? She never returned a phone call or nothing! Look! I mean, as you can see, I'm dang near irresistible."

"Evan, you're more than resistible," Michelle said. "You're despicable! You know good and well that you were more than just friends with that singer. And if you don't leave right now, the cops are going to be here any minute to take you away."

He unsnapped the holder for his knife, pulled it out and pointed it at us.

"We'll see about that, hot stuff. Don't make a move," he said.

But all three of us moved and looked outside as sirens filled the air, accompanied by the presence of blue lights in the front of the house. Two car doors closed and moments later a rapid knock sounded on the door, accompanied by voices identifying themselves as Metro Police.

Evan's thick-tongued voice declared confidently, "I'll just tell them I caught your boyfriend breaking in and they'll run him in instead of me. Ha!"

He opened the door with one hand and held the knife out at the officers standing at the door.

"Drop the knife, sir," one officer commanded while the other placed his hand on his service weapon.

"Wait! That guy over there broke in and I captured him, officer," Evan said in a slurred, broken speech.

"No! He's the one who broke in!" Michelle shouted, pointing at Evan. "I'm the one who called 911!"

One officer knocked the knife out of Evan's hand and quickly handcuffed him.

"Are you two okay?" the second officer asked.

"Yes, we're fine," Michelle said as she moved to me and held me close.

"Tell us what happened," he said.

"We had just come home from out of town and found him lying on the couch. Then I called 911. He pulled the knife on us just before you came in. Thank goodness you got here so fast."

"We were two blocks away on routine patrol when we got the call," he answered.

The officer who handcuffed Evan opened the door and led him out. The other said, "We're gonna take this guy to the station. You two will need to come by and press charges. Say, aren't you Max Jackson, the PI?"

"In the flesh, officer. Your boy here's got too much liquor on board and an even more ego. We'll see you at the station shortly."

The two officers exited the house with Evan in tow.

Michelle quickly turned and locked the door then leaned back against it as they left, a look of disbelief on her face.

"Your old boyfriend sure knows how to slam the brakes on a romantic moment," I said.

"He wasn't a boyfriend! He just thought that. We met at a mutual friend's album-release party. He hung out with me during the event and we went out for drinks with a group afterwards. We did go out a couple of times with some friends, but never just the two of us. It didn't take long for me to figure out he was nowhere near my type."

"So, what's with the M&M sign, and how'd he break in?"

"You see, once when this group was out together, we went to a thrift store looking for something we could use as Halloween costumes. While there, one of my friends spotted that neon green sign with the letters M&M."

Michelle nodded at the cursive M&M letters hanging on the front window.

"I found out it was originally made for Moore and Montgomery, an old manufacturing company somewhere. I thought it was cool looking, and since it was my initials, I bought it. It's one of a kind!"

"Yep, the kind that led your crazy friend right to your house," I said. "But back to my other question. How'd he get in?"

"You know that statue in the back?" she asked.

"Oh yeah—the nude pouring water from the urn? Did you model for it or is that just my imagination running wild?"

"Max! Can you be serious for a moment? Huh! Men! Sometimes y'all drive me crazy!" Michelle said.

"It's a mutual experience, sweetheart. Now go on."

"The pool is just outside my bathroom window. Sometimes in the summer, I open the window because I like to hear the water splash. It reminds me of a mountain stream in the Smokies and puts me right to sleep. I guess I left the window open the other night and forgot to lock it back."

"Michelle, I know this is a nice part of town, but you've got to be more careful for your own safety! You have a gated driveway, but it would be easy just to climb over the front fence. I hope you'll be more careful after this."

"I will for sure! I don't want anything like that to ever happen again," she said. "Hey, Max? About our together time? This whole break-in thing has been pretty nerve wracking." She sounded as disappointed as I was. "How about we take a rain check?"

"Sure, Michelle. I need to start writing my report for barrister Kubrick about Cassie, anyway."

"How's it going to go, if I might ask?"

"I hope I find that out when I write it," I said. "One minute Cassie seems just fine, and the next … well, I've got my doubts."

"I'm sure you'll do the right thing," Michelle said as she gave me a nice kiss on the cheek and walked with me to the door.

"Till next time?" she asked.

"Yeah. Maybe next time will be exciting in a different kind of way," I said, thinking about what might have been if that damn Evan hadn't shown up.

Chapter Twenty-one

When I arrived home, I noticed a large branch had fallen down in the backyard, and I went out to pick it up. Colonel Canyon was on his porch reading something—probably military history, his favorite subject. I thought Thursday morning was when he volunteered at the animal shelter, but here he was.

"Well at least you're walking straight, party animal, so I guess it couldn't have been too bad a night," he rumbled. "Looks to me like you could use a shave though, Jackson. How do you expect your sweet thing to show any interest in you the way you look? In my day, beard stubble and sloppy didn't get it with the girls. You look like crap, son."

I laughed. "Good mornin' to you too, Colonel Canyon. The party went great, and I apologize that I haven't made time to get cleaned up this morning. But you can bet I'll be ready for inspection by lunchtime!"

He laughed and said, "There won't be any inspection, but I would like some company for lunch and help with a little project. I got a pound of fresh 'cue from Sam's Barbeque Emporium this morning. Got coleslaw, baked beans, cornbread and chips to go with it. Why don't you come over and help me finish it off so I don't eat the whole thing?"

"I'll be glad to. See ya soon!" I said. That sausage biscuit for breakfast was long gone, and I was getting hungry.

There's something about taking a cool shower on a hot day. The water was refreshing, and it served the double purpose of helping me wake up, given that last night's quality of sleep was marginal at best.

After my shower, I threw on some jeans and a t-shirt and went next door to help Colonel Canyon. He opened the front door just as I was about to knock.

"What can I help you with, Colonel?"

I'd never been in the colonel's place before and was surprised to see a large set of workout equipment in the same area of the house that I used for an office. An opened cardboard box from Superior Gym Equipment rested on the floor in the hallway near where he stood.

"I got this punching speed-bag attachment for the workout set in the mail today and need you to hold the metal base while I attach it. Here. Grab this piece and line up the holes in the plate with the piece up there. Hold it while I secure the bolts."

Using a ratchet set and some nuts and bolts, he positioned the frame and tightened the new attachment in just a few minutes. He put down the tools, took a few practice punches at it, and seemed pleased with the addition.

"This is going to be great," he said. "Back in the day, I was a Golden Gloves champ in my age group. Even did some boxing in the service. I can't wait to start wearing this thing out," he said as he gave the bag another whack.

After double-checking that everything was assembled properly, we headed for the kitchen. The colonel placed all the sides on the table and warmed up the barbeque in the microwave. I put ice in glasses and poured us some Coke, and then we started lunch.

"So you been doing any sleuthing lately?" he asked.

"Yep. I'm trying to help a man determine if a relative is worthy of receiving a large inheritance. I just have to check this person out and make sure she's more or less walking the straight and narrow," I told him, careful not to mention any names.

"Whacha figured out so far? Is she going to be the lucky winner or will she have to keep working her butt off to help make ends meet like the rest of you workin' stiffs?" he asked.

"This one will likely keep working her butt off—literally and figuratively—no matter what happens. She's dedicated to her business and staying healthy, seems to basically care for her family, and does a few charitable things. On the other hand, she seems to be around when bad things happen to other family members who could potentially get the inheritance. She's been hanging around with one cousin who I know is a questionable character, been checking out sporty cars, and I think she may have accidentally almost killed my girlfriend by over-exercising her and then giving her a blood pressure pill to help with another issue."

There it was! I'd just summarized part of my report for Josef Kubrick in a few sentences. Now all I needed to do was to add some details and give him my recommendation.

"That's kind of a mixed bag of information you've got there, Sherlock, but I'm sure you'll figure it out," the colonel said as he sopped up the last of the barbecue sauce off his plate with a piece of cornbread.

"Yep. That's what I'm on my way to do now. Thanks for lunch! I hope you enjoy the new punching bag!" I said. I shook his hand and let myself out.

I took a shortcut through a gap in the boxwoods between our homes and headed for my office to write my summary before I forgot what I'd just told the colonel. The office was officially a second bedroom, but it only had a desk with a lamp, a chair and a few random photos on the wall that I'd recently framed. It was a quiet space that looked out over the front yard, with a view of the houses on my street. This afternoon, some kids were playing basketball in the driveway next door.

I lit a candle and started writing the draft.

Josef Kubrick, Esq.:

First of all, thank you for enlisting me for the personal analysis of Cassie Simpshire. I hope my findings will be helpful to you and your client.

Cassie seems to be fairly typical of women her age, although perhaps more motivated about some things in life than others. She's definitely driven to make her store profitable, makes plenty of time to stay in shape, and seems to have several friends. It's difficult to tell how serious her long-distance relationship with her boyfriend is, but it's still going on, so there's that. She doesn't seem to have too many really close friends, but still she has company for dinner, exercises with some women regularly, etc. Cassie has a heart for others and volunteers with a couple of charitable groups and, strangely enough, seems to want to help rehabilitate one of her cousins, Gabriel, who gives me a headache. With a history of little family harmony, she seems to want better relationships among the family, but I'm not sure how successful she'll be. At least she's trying.

Her relationship with her father is strained to the point that she thinks he could be spying on her through some kind of technological means, so she communicates with her boyfriend through snail mail using a friend as a go-between for sending and delivering. Her mother is not a strong influence. Cassie and I have a mutual friend, Michelle, who works near me and who speaks highly of her as a friend.

Concerns? There's nothing too incriminating, so I'll call it circumstantial evidence. She physically wore out my friend Michelle in an exercise class, gave her coffee and then a diuretic, which landed Michelle in the emergency room for dehydration. She made poppyseed casserole for cousin Gabriel the night before he got pulled over for evading arrest. Granted, he ran from the cops and had marijuana in the truck, but the opioid substance in his blood may have been from the poppyseed ... or could have been another source. She also shopped with Sammy Simpshire in Atlanta when he was arrested for theft from a jewelry store. Who knows? Perhaps she placed the ring in Sammy's pocket so he'd get picked up.

It may be that none of these events are important. Maybe Cassie didn't know the combination of things were potentially life-threatening to Michelle. Maybe the poppyseed wasn't the source of a positive test for Gabriel. Maybe Sammy really did steal the ring.

And since Cassie knows about her uncle's illness, I wonder if any of these actions are her way of making sure she's in on the inheritance and others are out. I've also caught her and cousin Gabriel shopping at a Porsche dealership since she got a letter about her uncle's illness. I wonder about that, too.

In summary, I'd like to think that Cassie Simpshire is a decent human being and is more deserving than any other family members I've run into or heard about. I had the opportunity to speak with her at a party recently and didn't detect a subversive nature in our conversation. I also trust the feminine intuition of my friend Michelle, who really likes Cassie and considers her a friend.

So from my perspective, and weighing all the information available, I would advise your client that Cassie Simpshire is a good person to receive the inheritance. Honoring the bassoons in the orchestra or roses at the botanical gardens would be nice, but if it were me, I'd pass it on to a real live human being in my family.

Sincerely,

Max Jackson

I read over the document several times and emailed it to Josef Kubrick. It would be interesting to hear what he thought about it and whether he agreed.

The sound of basketballs being dribbled outside beckoned me to join the teen boys playing next door. They often let me play since there weren't too many kids their age around, and my joining made teams even. After an hour of shooting hoops in the hot sun, I was done.

I took off my shirt and found a towel in the bathroom to wipe my sweat off. Cruising through the kitchen, still patting myself dry, I noticed a missed call on my phone and a voicemail from Josef Kubrick, Esquire.

Chapter Twenty-two

"Give me a call, Jackson! I need to talk to you!" Josef's voice boomed through the phone.

I called him back and he picked up immediately.

"Jackson! It's a good thing you got that report to me. I was getting a little concerned that I wasn't even a blip on your radar! Although I must admit, it looks like you did a thorough job of getting information about Cassie. I'll get my new secretary to type it on our office letterhead and make it look official before I send it to Mr. Deere. It's a good report, but I'm not sure how he'll take it."

"He can take it anyway he wants to. I just did what you asked me to do, and now I'm looking forward to being paid for it. So, when will I see the other 10K?" I asked.

"This weekend, my good man. As you know, Mr. Deere is having a big party at his mansion in Buckhead. I'll send you the address. You and a date just got an invitation, compliments of me. I know the party's mainly about football for family and friends, but with this guy and the situation he's in, I'm afraid he might say something about his illness. But then, he wouldn't want to spoil the mood at a Georgia football game party. Especially with his family there. They're all invited. The shindig starts at eleven Eastern; game starts at noon. It's one of those awful early games. Remember to wear something with Georgia red and black. He's old school and wants everyone to dress up, so get yourself a tie and a jacket. When I see you at the party, I'll hand you an envelope with the balance of your payment inside. Oh! And send me a bill with all your travel expenses. The old man says you're on the payroll. How's that sound?"

"Sounds better and better. I'll check about my date, but count me in for sure," I answered, wondering if Michelle would be up for yet another party this week. At least she won't be in charge of this one.

Then it hit me: *how in the heck would we explain to Cassie why we were at her uncle's party*! Very strange coincidence? Mutual friends? Just happened to be in the neighborhood? Whatever reason I came up with would have to be good, because Cassie was sharp enough to see right through some half-baked excuse.

I touched my phone for Michelle's mobile number and hoped she was around.

"Miss me already?" Michelle said as she answered.

"Now that I think about it, sure, but that's not the reason I'm calling," I said. "Turns out, Claude Deere is having a big party for the Georgia game on Saturday at his mansion in Atlanta. The pregame starts at eleven, and kickoff is at noon. And we're invited! The only catch is that you have to wear Georgia colors and go with me."

"That sounds like fun, Max! But when do we leave, and how do we get there? For that matter, when will we come home? I'll need to make sure I have the right thing to wear. Is it dressy or casual?" she asked anxiously.

"Thinking out loud, I'd say we catch a ridiculously early flight Saturday —though, no, I don't have tickets yet—and then we'll call an Uber to get to a house that I don't yet have an address for, and I haven't even thought about where we'll stay. The dress code is dressy, whatever that is for women. I know I have to wear a sport coat with a tie that's gonna be hot as hell on an early September afternoon in Atlanta." I couldn't remember the last time I wore a coat and tie in summer.

"I know just what I'll wear! It'll be a surprise and I know you'll love it," she said. "So, will we know anyone at this party?"

"Evidently he's invited family members and some friends that are Georgia fans. So besides me, you can bet Cassie will be there and maybe Gabriel, if he doesn't find a way to get arrested between now and then. I'll let you know ASAP when I get things worked out about our travel plans."

I paused for a second. "And I'm really glad you can come with me, Michelle, especially on such short notice. You know, you're not too bad to hang around with."

"Not too bad, huh? That's quite a compliment coming from you, Max. Well it's only fair. I dragged you into Wednesday's party on the spur of the moment, and now you're offering me a similar invitation except you're not putting me to work. Yesterday's event turned out fine, after a while, and I'm sure this one will, too!"

Michelle always had a way of finding the positives in situations. I was looking forward to having her company in Atlanta.

"Terrific! I'll call you when I get things worked out. See ya!"

I fired up my MacBook to check on round-trip Nashville-to-Atlanta flights leaving Saturday morning. There were a few early ones that were pricey, but I was on the Deere payroll, so no big deal. Just as I was about to secure my plane reservation, my phone rang. I answered.

"Jackson? This is O'Hara. Got a minute?"

Sergeant O'Hara's voice sounded distant, and the background sound of a car engine made it a little hard to understand what he was saying.

"Sure! Hang on one second while I finish something," I said.

I made a couple of clicks on the computer and the flight reservations were done.

"Thanks for letting me wrap that up, O'Hara. What's up?"

"We found out who killed the Maserati driver," he said with a degree of satisfaction.

"That's great news! Was he wanted? What's the story?"

"You're not going to believe this, Jackson. A guy came down to the precinct and said he wanted to talk to someone about the shooting. He was in an interrogation room with me and a detective, and he told me that he was sighting-in his rifle that afternoon in his backyard, a couple of blocks off Hobbs. He had the gun on a stand pointed at a target in front of a hillside on his property. Evidently he did it often enough that the neighbors were used to the noise. This time, however, just as he was about to shoot, some big ole stray dog ran into him and knocked the gun barrel to where it pointed toward the highway. The shot went through two wooded backyards and then out to the street, where it hit the guy driving down the road. Talk about a one-in-a-million shot."

"That's unbelievable, O'Hara. What's gonna happen to the shooter?"

"I don't know. That's up to the DA. The guy's no threat to society as far as I can see, but it was his fault," O'Hara said.

"Well at least you know what happened. It wasn't anything malicious, gang-related, or premeditated. Just a really unfortunate accident."

"Yep. Well, now you know."

He continued.

"By the way, Jackson, some of my friends will be at our favorite watering hole this Tuesday evening celebrating my birthday. Want to join us?"

"I'll try to make it, O'Hara. Thanks for the invitation! See you Tuesday."

I made a quick note about the Tuesday gathering on a sticky-pad, stuck it on the refrigerator and proceeded to finalize plans for the weekend.

After a while, I completed the hotel reservations. I typed out an itinerary for Michelle and emailed it to her so she could check it out. I wondered how she'd react to me picking her up at 5:30 AM Saturday morning to catch the flight. I guess I'd find out what kind of bird she was; early or otherwise.

My phone buzzed with a text message—the address for Claude Deere was 1 Grand Vista Ridge Estates. Now I knew where we were headed. Sounded like a snazzy place to me!

Chapter Twenty-three

Friday

I finally found just the right attire for the party at the Sports Gear Casuals store: an official University of Georgia tie imprinted with a silver-studded collar bulldog. That and a basic white shirt, a black sport coat and khakis would complete my outfit. Pants and a shirt were already in the closet, so the only thing that set me back was the tie and sport coat. I figured I might get some mileage out of the sport coat. The tie? It probably wouldn't ever see the light of day again.

With Cassie's case more or less behind me, I turned to other work matters at hand, which unfortunately was nothing. I had no other job begging for my attention. My desk was bare as the Kroger bread aisle after a snowstorm forecast in Nashville. I hadn't gotten the first piece of mail all week—not even a credit-card application or a "bundle my home and auto insurance" offer (as if nobody had ever heard of that before). My inbox was cluttered with advertisements and fall specials from Home Depot and Lowes among others.

Since it was lunchtime and I didn't have anything else to do, I decided to try a new restaurant in the Gulch. I heard they served homestyle—meat and three types of vegetables. Like most of the new restaurants around here, it got very popular fast and was successful—or at least till the newness wore off.

On the way there, I heard sirens behind me, and glancing in the rearview mirror, I saw a hook-and-ladder fire truck whipping around the corner at the intersection of 12th and Edgehill about a block behind me. I pulled over to let it pass, then spied its likely destination: a plume of smoke coming several blocks away toward downtown. There was so much construction downtown, I figured the fire had to be related to a new building going up. After the firetruck passed, traffic moved back into their regular lanes.

I followed the truck as it headed straight down 12th, then spotted a police car and an ambulance ahead. As I approached my lunch destination in the Gulch, smoke grew thicker, with red flashing lights everywhere. Traffic was blocked at the street where I needed to turn, so I pulled into a parking lot close enough to the restaurant and walked briskly toward the scene of the fire to see what was happening.

About a block from the fire, I saw firemen pulling hoses and carrying fire extinguishers from trucks toward the place on fire. The smoke was thick, but the fire wasn't what I'd call out of control. When I turned the corner, I saw smoke billowing out the front door of Winner's Threads. *Cassie's store!*

Firemen donned their masks and rushed inside. Bystanders like me watched with interest as other emergency vehicles pulled into the area. It seemed like everyone had their phones out, recording the event. One firetruck directed a stream of water toward the back part of the building's roof, where most of the smoke was coming from. A whoosh of steam rose toward the sky and water sizzled as it doused the flames. The air had that aroma of a burning campfire being put out, except the concentration was much greater and almost made me choke as I took in a breath.

By this time, police had rerouted traffic from the area and motioned for folks, including me, to back away from the scene. As we retreated, a guy next to me pointed to the building and exclaimed, "Look! They're bringing somebody out!"

I looked toward the store entrance and sure enough, they were. I figured the person would be a customer in the store, but when I looked closer, I saw that it was Cassie. She had an oxygen mask over her mouth and nose and was walking out pretty much on her own power, although her arms were draped over the shoulders of two firemen for extra support. They took her nearby to an ambulance and sat her on the curb. She didn't appear to be burned.

I made my way around the block where I could get closer to her and see how she was. The police barricade didn't reach the ambulance, so I walked over to Cassie like I was supposed to be there.

"You need to step back, sir," one of the paramedics told me.

"I'm a friend of Cassie's," I said. "Is she okay?"

Cassie raised her head, looked at me, nodded a yes and waved me to come over.

"She's gonna be fine," the paramedic said. "She got a little smoke inhalation trying to put out the fire, but she's responding well to the oxygen."

I knelt down in front of Cassie, focused on her and smiled, trying to give her some comfort. Her eyes, already red from the smoke, glanced toward the store and started to tear up. She looked back at me then folded forward, her head in her hands, elbows on knees.

"Any idea what happened?" I asked in the general direction of the paramedics.

Cassie pulled the mask off her face. She coughed a few times and cleared her throat.

"I can tell you. Somebody tried to burn the place down! I was folding t-shirts at the front of the store by the summer sale table when I heard a noise in the warehouse area behind me. It was a crash—like glass breaking—then an explosion. I ran back and saw flames on a pile of clothes that had just come in yesterday! Some of the clothes were on fire, but it was almost like flames were burning on top of the clothes. That was so weird! The window that faces the alley was broken and glass was everywhere. I found a jacket nearby and tried to beat out the flames, but all that did was make things worse."

She paused to catch her breath, then continued.

"Then I remembered the fire extinguisher mounted on the wall nearby and ran to get it. I came back to the fire, pointed the nozzle, pulled the pin, squeezed the handle and only got one spray of stuff. I looked at it wondering what I was doing wrong and saw the needle on the pressure dial pointing to 'Discharged'. No wonder it didn't work. I never thought that I'd use that thing. I never thought to check.... everything I've been working for up in flames..."

She coughed and started sobbing again. The paramedic nearest her encouraged her to rest and to put the mask back on. She nodded and replaced the mask, still crying.

"Anything I can do? I asked.

"Since she wasn't burned and she's breathing okay, there's really no reason for her to go to the hospital. It would be good to have somebody watch her for a while when she gets home."

"We have a mutual friend who'll be just right for that. I'll be glad to take her home."

Cassie took off her mask again and said, "I'll need my purse and leather satchel. They're under the counter near the cash register."

"I think I can get your purse, but until the investigation is over, I don't think they'll want us moving too much around," the paramedic said. "Don't worry, someone will be here till the inspectors finish their work, and then they'll lock it up." He seemed pleased that his patient was okay and that the mid-day's excitement was just about over.

I gave Michelle a call, told her a brief summary of what happened and asked if she could help. She said she'd meet us at Cassie's apartment in about fifteen minutes.

By now, fire hoses were being rolled up and reloaded onto the trucks. Emergency vehicles started to leave the area, and curious onlookers dispersed as the scene calmed down. The air was still smoky and water continued to trickle out the front door. Thank goodness the fire had been a small one and that the Nashville Fire Department got it under control so quickly.

A paramedic came back with Cassie's purse and satchel and asked once again if she was all right. She gave assurance that she was, then stood and turned toward me to leave.

"What about your car, Cassie? You can't leave it here all night, can you?" I asked.

"Actually, it's in the shop. I took an Uber to work this morning, so no worries. Can you bring your car around? For once in my life, I really don't feel like walking very far," she said, still taking short breaths as she recovered from inhaling smoke.

"Sure," I answered. "Hang tight right here. I'm parked just a block away, so I won't be long."

I thought. *Who would want to burn down Cassie's business?* Was it some random act of violence? Somebody trying to get back at her? Threaten her? I wanted to find out more, but job one was to get Cassie out of there and at home where she could rest.

After I picked her up and we started down the road, I noticed that Cassie reeked of smoke, which was no surprise. During whatever time she spent in the store during the fire, smoke had saturated her clothes, her hair, and whatever else it could cling to. I rolled down the back windows and ran the AC on medium to keep the air cool and fresh.

Cassie stared straight ahead on the ride to her place, despondent, and generally quiet. She mumbled something about calling the insurance company. Then she talked about how long it would be until she could get the store open again, and wondered if her old customers would come back.

I thought about the fact that I was driving with the subject of an investigation I'd just completed. It felt kind of strange knowing that I had been learning all about her, and now she was trusting me as a friend. She certainly didn't have an attitude like, "Oh well, my store just burned, but I'm getting ready to inherit millions, so no biggie." She was genuinely bummed. It was pretty obvious that the store was her baby and she'd put her heart and soul into it. Inheritance or not.

"I guess you know where I live," she said, referring to my recent experience there with Gabriel.

"Sure do. Did I tell you Michelle's going to meet us here and plans to keep you company for a while?"

"I heard you talk about a mutual friend with the paramedic and figured that's who you meant. That's nice of her to come. I really appreciate the two of you taking care of me, Max."

She paused and breathed a deep sigh.

"And on top of all, I've got a party in Atlanta to go to tomorrow. Most of my dysfunctional family will be there. There's no way I can miss it, though. But this fire is a big huge thing, and they'll just have to understand why I couldn't come. I better call my Uncle Claude now and let him know."

I thought to myself that if Cassie wasn't going to the party, I wouldn't have to make up some crazy reason why I was at the same party.

She reached for her phone and dialed a number. A deep male voice answered.

"Hello?"

"Uncle Claude. This is Cassie. I want to let you know that there's been a fire at my business here in Nashville, and I won't be able to make the party tomorrow. I'm so sorry. I really wanted to come," she said apologetically.

She paused and listened as Uncle Claude offered his concern about the fire and encouraged her not to change her plans, according to what little I could make of the conversation.

"Sure," she answered. "You're right. There's not much I can do about it tomorrow."

She listened again.

"Thanks for your concern and good advice," she said. "You always were the wisest one in the family."

Cassie looked over at me as she spoke and said, "Thank you. Okay. I'll be there tomorrow as planned."

Evidently Uncle Claude had something else to say that I couldn't make out as she continued the conversation.

"Oh, I'll be fine. A friend picked me up and is taking me home where our mutual friend, Michelle, is going to stay with me this afternoon."

Cassie listened.

"Really! Why, that's so kind! I'll check and see. Bye now!"

"Max, you won't believe this. You and Michelle just scored an invitation to my Uncle Claude's party in Atlanta tomorrow afternoon!"

Chapter
Twenty-four

"My Uncle Claude is so grateful for you and Michelle taking care of me that he wants you to come to his shindig this weekend. There's a big Georgia football game, and he's having a gathering of family and friends for a pre-game party at his home. It's a really nice place! Really nice!"

She paused.

"I know this is, like, super short notice, but do you think you two could go?" Cassie asked.

I couldn't believe my ears. Now I had a legit reason for being at her uncle's house tomorrow!

By now, Cassie had broken out of her funk about the fire and had something to look forward to. Mention of the party certainly perked her up.

"We'd love to go, Cassie. In fact, Michelle and I had already planned a trip to Atlanta this weekend, but I'm sure we can make time for your uncle's party. What do I need to know about it?"

"It starts at eleven in the morning since the game is a noon kickoff, dress code is dressy, and you need to wear Georgia red and black. The address is 1 Grand Vista Ridge Estates in Buckhead. His home sits on a hill which faces town. Believe me, everybody in Buckhead knows my uncle's place! You won't have any trouble finding it. There's like a million roses on the ravine in the front yard facing the highway. It will be an incredible sight to see, although many have already bloomed by now."

We pulled into the front of Cassie's apartment and saw Michelle already waiting out front. She had a brown bag in hand from her favorite restaurant and had a look of concern on her face for her friend. She ran out to the road and opened the car door for Cassie.

"I got here as fast as I could! Are you okay?" she asked as she gave Cassie a hug. "I heard about the fire and was worried. When Max called, I was on my way to pick up lunch from

Nguyen's Vietnamese Take Out. I figured you'd be hungry so I got two orders," offered Michelle.

"Thanks, Michelle. I am kind of hungry. And I need a shower and clean clothes. Eeeeew!" said Cassie as she took a sniff of her hair and made a disgusted face. "I smell like I've been sitting in front of a campfire. I hope I didn't ruin your car, Max."

As we walked toward the house, I remembered that Michelle hadn't heard about our second invitation to the same party and needed to know soon.

"Hey Michelle! Cassie's uncle in Atlanta is so grateful for us taking care of her that he's invited us to a Georgia pre-game party tomorrow. And we'd already planned to go to Atlanta this weekend! Isn't that a coincidence?"

Michelle gave me the oddest look and fortunately caught my wink and fake smile encouraging her to play along.

"How nice, Cassie! Woohoo! I love an SEC football party!" said Michelle.

I smiled at Michelle. Her response was Oscar-worthy and even had me convinced that she was excited about it.

I said goodbye to the women as they went upstairs to Cassie's apartment, then headed back to my place. One the way home, I wondered what the next day would bring and hoped Cassie would be as excited about going to Atlanta as she seemed this afternoon.

Chapter Twenty-five

Saturday

When I went to collect Michelle, she was right on time and looked fabulous. Not everyone could pull off looking so great at five-thirty in the morning. She carried a small red-plaid bag with her purse strapped over her shoulder. Since I only had one bag, we wouldn't need to check luggage, which would save us a bunch of time on our tight schedule. Michelle tossed her bag next to mine in the backseat, hopped into the car, and we took off. With the airport thirty minutes away at most and light traffic, I figured we'd make our flight easily.

"Mornin' Max! Ready for a big day?" she said as she hopped in.

"Big? Like, large? More day than yesterday?" I answered.

"I mean a good one, with fun things to do, excitement, a day we'll remember—that kind of big." Then she punched me on the arm.

"Ouch! Yeah, I'm looking forward to it, too! Traveling with you, going to the party, watching the game, getting paid for my work on the case, being with you tonight…"

Michelle reached her hand over to lovingly touch my arm where she punched it as I drove.

"And I'm looking forward to being with you, too," she said with a smile.

I kept my eyes on the road, but could sense her big blues looking in my direction as she spoke. Yes, this was going to be a good weekend.

After parking the car and riding a shuttle back to the terminal, we made our way to the Southwest Airlines boarding area and got in line with the other early morning passengers. It always amazed me how no matter the time of day, there were always a ton of people coming and going at the airport, as if morning and night didn't matter when it came to catching planes and returning home.

Once we boarded the plane, it was obvious that our flight was going to be full. I didn't spot Cassie as a fellow passenger, but supposed she could have already boarded and been in the back. Michelle sat next to a window and I sat in the middle seat, sandwiched between her and a guy who turned out to be a boat salesman on his way to a convention. While he was trying to interest me in a new Mastercraft X Series boat, I noticed he kept checking out Michelle. She did look very nice, but as it turned out, she wasn't much interested in a boat, either. Seeing that a sale wasn't going to happen, he put some sound-cancelling headphones over his ears and picked out one of the magazines in the seat pocket to read.

Now that we had a little bit of privacy, Michelle leaned over and said, "I've been meaning to tell you something, Max. You know when you came to my house that first time, and I told you about my winning lottery ticket?"

"I remember. What happened?"

"Well, I went to a friend's Christmas get-together a couple of years ago where they gave chocolate covered pretzels along with a Tennessee Lottery ticket as party favors. I never play the lottery, so I didn't really know how it worked. One day a week or so afterwards, a friend who was also at the party asked if I had checked my ticket to see if I had a winner. I hadn't, but when I got home, I scratched off the ticket and discovered that mine matched printed numbers on the ticket! I still wasn't sure what to do, so I called the number for the lottery office and talked to someone who told me I'd won! It wasn't like one of those really huge payouts, but the million-dollar prize was certainly nice."

She placed her hand next to her mouth and whispered to me as she said, "million dollar."

"I felt bad since the people who gave the party actually bought the ticket, so I sent them a thank you note and a nice check of appreciation. At the time, I was in an apartment paying ridiculous rent, so I decided it would be a good investment to buy a house. I had to put a lot aside for taxes, but still had enough to buy the house and fix it up. I also paid off my student loans and put some in savings. I guess if everyone gets one lucky day, I got mine."

"What a great story! Maybe some of your good luck will rub off on me. Say, I'm curious what Cassie will do with her inheritance if she gets it. Maybe that new Porsche will become a reality."

"Do you think she'd really buy one?" Michelle asked.

"Who knows? Maybe she was just looking. Or maybe Gabriel made her go."

The flight to Atlanta took a little over an hour. It was smooth and easy. After we landed, we maneuvered our way through the airport to get to the passenger pickup. I had pre-booked an Uber before we left and got a message saying the car —a deep blue Mercedes Benz C-Class sedan—was on its way. The driver's name was Ulysses and he spoke four languages: English, French, German and Spanish.

After waiting a short while, a car fitting the description with a lighted Uber sign on the dash pulled up next to the curb. Odd thing was, judging from the plastic sign strapped on top of his car, he was also a pizza delivery guy. In a Benz, no less!

Ulysses got out, welcomed us to Atlanta, and said he'd be taking care of us on our trip to Buckhead. He opened the trunk, but we opted to keep our minimal luggage in the back seat with us. While the trunk was still open, I noticed a metal box bolted to the trunk floor. When we got going, I couldn't resist and had to ask him about it.

"That's where I keep the pizza," he said. "I installed the box - a low watt oven to keep the pizzas warm, just about one hundred degrees. People love getting a warm pizza delivered," he said confidently. "When I'm not driving Uber, I do deliveries for a local pizza chain. When not delivering pizza, I deliver people. Sometimes I do both! Keeps me busy, too. I have some customers say when they get in, that they love the aroma of pizza. A rider last week asked me to drop him off at the pizza place instead of where he was planning to go for dinner!"

"That's cool!" I answered. "Now, what's the deal with the Benz? You must be the only Uber driver in the country with a Mercedes Benz! Doesn't that turn off your clients?" I said, thinking that customers might question a rich Uber driver.

"Not at all. It's a fine ride and frankly, folks like arriving at their destination in a fancy car! I work hard for my 4.9 Uber score and every little thing I can do to make a nice ride for my customers benefits me. Truth is, I got an incredible deal for this beaut on Ebay for next to nothing. All it needed to get runnin' right was a little love and a $1,500 fuel injector," he said like a man who was part mechanic and knew a deal when he saw one.

Atlanta traffic was crazy as usual, with cars everywhere, going in all directions at a pretty good clip. Riding or driving in Atlanta always made me think this was what being in a NASCAR race was like. Guided by his GPS, Ulysses got us to our hotel in about forty minutes. He pulled into the hotel check-in lane, let us out, and wished us a good day. It was easy to see why he had such a good rating from his customers.

It had been a few hours since my early morning Cheerios, and his mention of pizza had made me hungry. However, we were supposed to have lunch at the party, so I restrained myself from getting a snack and decided to wait.

Check-in at the hotel was a piece of cake since Cassie's uncle made our hotel the recommended place to stay for out-of-towners and arranged for early check-in. Our room was on the thirty-fifth floor and had a breathtaking view of downtown. The king-sized bed had more pillows on it than I thought two people would ever use.

After a quick look around the room, Michelle excused herself to freshen up and get dressed. I went ahead and unpacked what little I brought, then changed into my clothes for the party. Since I wasn't a Georgia fan, I felt a little odd wearing their school colors—especially the tie with a cute, slobbering bulldog mascot.

While I was admiring the view of downtown, the next breathtaking sight walked out of the bathroom. Michelle had redone her hair and wore a red pleated slip dress trimmed in black that twirled as she spun around on her white strappy sandals.

"I take it by your gaping mouth that you like the dress," she said, smiling.

"You look beautiful, Michelle. I mean, beautiful! You're going to be the prettiest southern belle at the party this afternoon," I said. It brought to mind lyrics to an old Beatles tune, but I figured she'd probably heard the reference too many times to be charmed by the mention.

"You look nice, too, Max. Hey. What's this on the dresser?" she said as she picked up and opened a small card addressed to Max and Michelle.

"Thank you for coming to my pre-game party! Enclosed, you'll find the itinerary, address and directions to my home. In addition, below is your code for a complimentary Uber ride to the party and back if you need one.

Go Dawgs!"
- C. Deere

"Well, isn't that nice," Michelle said. "This uncle of Cassie's really knows how to entertain." She held up the invitation. "The party starts at eleven. We'd better call this number and get a move on. I don't want to miss a minute of it!"

It was about a ten minute drive to Cassie's uncle's place. When we arrived at the address, a short line of cars waited outside the entrance to the gated community of Grand Vista Ridge Estates. Large ornate iron gates separated the private property from the public. The entrance to the road was monitored by a pair of ripped security guards wearing Polo shirts with 'Elite Security' stitched on the chest pocket. As each car entered, I noticed that the first guard spoke to the driver or back seat passenger, and the other opened the gate when he got a signal from the first.

When it was our turn the guard asked me, "Good morning, sir. Your names please?"

"Max Jackson, and this is Michelle McCartney."

He consulted his iPhone, made some kind of notation on it and called back to his partner, "They're good."

The gate started to open and in a matter-of-fact professional tone and a tip of the hat, he said, "You're checked in, sir Have a nice day and go Dawgs."

We nodded our heads and smiled as the Uber started up the long and winding road.

It turned out that only three houses were in Grand Vista Ridge Estates, each with what looked like at least thirty acres of property, beautifully manicured and filled with oak and pine trees, azaleas, and, on Claude's property—just as Cassie had described—one ravine with nothing but roses. It was breathtaking. Ubers dropped visitors at the main entrance under a pagoda covered in wisteria vine, which had shed some blooms, making a natural welcome carpet of purple for party-goers. People in their own cars were greeted by a valet who parked their cars for them.

As we got out of our car and approached the house, we saw the man I figured to be Claude Deere there at the front door, greeting guests as they arrived.

Claude smiled, extended his hand to me and said, "You must be Max Jackson, and this must be your lovely date, Michelle. I'm so glad you could make it!" He stepped back, looking at her, and said, "My, don't you do those Georgia colors proud!"

Chapter Twenty-six

*S*ince I'd never met or talked to Claude Deere, I was surprised that he called both of us by name.

We responded with a couple of "nice to meet yous" and returned the welcome.

"With all the people at this party, how'd you know our names, Mr. Deere?" I asked.

"Claude's the name, son. Just call me Claude. How'd I know it was you? That was easy. First of all, you didn't drive your own car, so I figured you weren't local. Secondly, Cassie sent me a selfie of her and Michelle at a coffee shop in Nashville, so I would know what she looked like. Obviously, you'd be her date. Mainly, I personally know everyone else I invited, so I figured you had to be Michelle and Max," he said with a smile. "Did you like how I got you a second invitation to the party so Cassie wouldn't be suspicious as to why you were here? Quick thinking, huh?" he said proudly.

"That is pretty sharp, Claude. We appreciate *both* invitations. And we'd better get inside so you can welcome these folks behind us."

Michelle and I entered through two large doors that were solid carved wood and bevelled glass to find a grand parlour with twin sweeping staircases on the left and right, rising from Italian marble floors and meeting at a second floor landing. Walls were adorned with Dutch Master-style paintings while several ornate loveseats and chairs scattered strategically about the place looked more like museum pieces than furniture for casual lounging. A huge chandelier hung from the ceiling with a hundred or more Pollyanna-like prisms, which with sunshine, illuminated the room in a spectrum of colors.

Despite the rainbow of colors' efforts to cheer up the grand entry hall, there were no photos of Claude with his wife, formal or otherwise, from places visited on vacation or fun times. No big group family photos were around either—just the finer things purchased by his wealth. It gave me a hollow feeling as I determined that it took more than a bunch of crystal clear prisms on a sunny day to brighten up a home.

Straight ahead, we saw a row of glass doors that opened out to a veranda where many of the guests had gathered. I figured the food was bound to be there, so I nudged Michelle that direction.

As we stepped through the doors outside, the warmth of a summer breeze hit us in contrast to the cool air inside the home. Several large fans kept air circulating to keep folks comfortable, but not enough to blow off the fancy hats in Georgia colors worn by some of the women.

Just as we expected, neither Michelle or I recognized a soul as we searched for Cassie in the room. Not finding her, we made our way to the hors d'oeuvres table and helped ourselves. Among other things, they had asparagus tips wrapped in bread with cream cheese inside and cocktail weiners simmering in barbecue sauce with red and black skewers in a crystal dish nearby for stabbing them.

While we were perusing the snacks, an older, rotund fellow dressed in a gaudy red-and-white striped sport coat with black lapels approached me. "Young man," he said a little tipsily, "who do *you* think was the best Georgia football player of all time?"

Going through my limited University of Georgia football knowledge, I answered him best I could. "I'd say Herschel Walker or maybe Champ Bailey. I guess I'd go with Herschel since he carried the ball. Offensive players seem to win all the 'best of' awards."

"My feelings exactly! Thank you very much."

He took another sip of his mint julep, turned and proceeded to the next group of men to ask the same question.

"Gentlemen, who do you think..."

Michelle and I found a corner at the part of the veranda furthest from the house and sat down to admire the view of the city. A little table nearby served to hold beer, soft drinks and plates of food. I got two of everything at the serving table cause I was starving. Check that; I took three weiners.

"This is the life!" I said as I placed my arm around Michelle and settled into the love seat.

"Yes, it's nice. But it's so big, and his wife is gone and there's no one to share it with. I mean, he probably looks out at the city from any number of places in this house wishing he could be a part of the fun people are having together in town. But he'd just be here in this big ole mansion, alone. I don't even think he's got a dog or an aquarium! He's bound to get lonely when he doesn't have guests around. Look, there's only a few people here that are his age. I'm not so sure this is the life I want," Michelle said.

"True. But at least he *has* friends. He probably likes to entertain, and today's football game is just the ticket. That's one way to break the loneliness." From what I saw, Claude seemed to be having a grand time this morning.

We looked back behind us at the entrance and saw several more guests arriving. The constant flow of red and black outfits was almost comical to me for a fancy affair at a mansion like this, but I guess it did add to the festive Georgia fan spirit.

Among the new arrivals was none other than our friend Cassie, apparently by herself, complete with a charming smile and wearing a short white dress with thin red sequin stripes and a red and black corsage pinned to her left shoulder. She looked much happier than the downhearted woman I saw at the fire yesterday.

It seemed like most everyone went to greet Cassie. Many of the guests approached her with handshakes or hugs, as though she were a prodigal daughter. After a while, she made her way through the crowd and to the refreshment table.

She took a sip of her drink and spotted Michelle waving to her from our end of the patio.

"Michelle! Max!" she shouted as she set down the drink and ran toward us quickly as she could in heels and a tight dress.

"I'm so glad you could make it! Have you met my Uncle Claude? Isn't he sweet?"

"We sure did," Michelle answered. "He even knew our names!"

"I don't know how he does it, but he's always been good with people and their names," commented Cassie. "That's probably one of the reasons he's been so successful."

She looked around the room and surveyed the crowd.

"Look at all the people! Oh my gosh! It looks like the riff-raff are here, too," she said, nodding across the room.

Cassie directed our attention to a group of several folks close to her age, congregated in an area near a big-screen TV watching *ESPN's College GameDay,* which was broadcast live from Athens. They seemed to be enjoying each other's company and not necessarily mixing with the rest of the crowd. Of course, neither were we.

"Who's the riff-raff?" I asked.

About that time, one person I did recognize, Gabriel Farasinni, joined the group and gave everyone a high-five. From the looks of things, he was in his element.

"That would be my ring-stealing cousin Sammy wearing the ball cap, my gold-digger cousin Layla with the dark tan and low-cut red-and-white dress standing next to whoever the guy is in the suit, and of course we all know Gabriel, who I see has found yet another opportunity to wear camo—the red and black version." Michelle sighed.

"I don't know who peed in our family gene pool, but I've got some real winners for cousins," she said.

We chuckled at the comment but I also felt sorry for her, since they obviously upset her. An overabundance of cousins she didn't really care for, each with their own set of problems, made family times difficult, which was probably why she moved away to Nashville.

Cousin Layla and her companion in the suit started over to where we were standing. When they arrived, Layla greeted Cassie with a put-on smile and gave her a big hug.

"Well if it isn't my successful cousin from Nashville! It's me, Layla! You need to come to Atlanta sometime and visit. Maybe catch a few rays too, girl. You sure could use some sun on that fit body of yours. I've got a cute little two-piece that would look so good on you," she said in a manner that caused Cassie to turn a little red.

"I'll keep that in mind," Cassie answered. "Who's your friend?" she asked as she nodded to the gentleman in the suit beside Layla.

"This, my dear cousin, is Josef Kubrick, Esquire—that means lawyer. We met recently right here in this very house and have pretty much been together ever since. He likes a younger woman and I like an older man. Josef, this is my cousin Cassie, and I don't know who these people are," she said pointing at Michelle and me.

WHAT?? *This is Josef Kubrick? Kubrick had a date with one of Cassie's cousins, a potential heir to the Deere fortune?*

Cassie nodded her head and said, "Nice to meet you, Josef. These are my friends Michelle McCartney and Max Jackson."

I swear the lawyer's mouth dropped when he heard my name. His demeanor changed as he smiled and put out his hand for me to shake.

"Small world, isn't it Max? It's nice to meet you in person," he said as he continued to shake and smile with the sincerity of a vacation time-share salesman.

Layla looked dumbfounded, pointed back and forth at the two of us and said, "So, like, you two, like, know each other?"

"I've done some business for Josef in Nashville recently," I answered hoping that would suffice for Layla and not make Cassie suspicious.

"As a matter of fact," Josef said as he pulled an envelope out of his suit coat pocket and handed it to me. "This is for you. And I want you to know that I'll be in Nashville on Tuesday. I'd like to meet with you and the lovely Michelle to discuss some unfinished business. Say, 7 PM at some out-of-the-way place in south Nashville?"

"Sure. Meet us at the Andy Jack Brewery on 21st. That's a good place for unfinished business meetings," I said as I took the envelope and put it in my inside chest pocket. I wondered exactly what business between us was unfinished. I couldn't help but sense the check for ten thousand dollars warming a spot in my coat. I so wanted to take a look at it, but resisted the urge.

Layla adjusted the strap of her dress and smacked her gum as she grabbed Josef's arm. "Let's go back over here where the action is, Sugar Daddy. I need another drink."

Cassie excused herself, too and went back to fetch the drink she had left on the table.

As they walked away, I asked quietly, "Michelle, did you catch that? Layla is one of Cassie's cousins and he's dating her as well as representing her uncle regarding his fortune. Doesn't that seem a little strange?"

"Oh my! That is odd. Why he could….."

As Michelle spoke, Claude Deere made his way to the middle of the large patio and clinked a spoon on an empty crystal water glass to get everyone's attention.

"Greetings, Georgia fans! First of all, thank all of you for coming to the party today. I want to personally predict that our Bulldogs are going to put a whoopin' on them boys from up north today and teach 'em how we play football down here!"

A big cheer rose from the guests.

"Before the game starts, I'd like to make an announcement. As you know, I lost my dear wife, Johnna, not too long ago, and as a result, this house, with reminders of her at each turn, has become more of a prison to me than a home. So, I'd like to announce that I've purchased a villa at Seniors Living Elite nearby and put the sale of this property in the capable hands of my dear friend Sharon of Sharon's Estates Realtors. Yes, I'm going to miss the rose garden, the view of the city, and all the memories these walls and I share. However, circumstances, I mean, well, it's just time for me to make the move."

He nodded his head briefly and blinked his eyes, then paused for the hushed conversation in the room as everyone took in this seemingly big news.

"Now, enough of this sentimental talk," he continued. "It's about time for kickoff! Go Dawgs!" he shouted as he did a fist pump in the air.

The crowd cheered again and dispersed to the serving table or a good seat near the seventy-two inch television in the corner of the room.

"He's a proud man, my uncle," said Cassie, who returned with her drink. "Always thinking of others and not looking for pity or personal favors. He's gonna miss this place." She wiped a tear from her eye.

Michelle eased over and gave her a gentle hug.

"Besides you, it sounds like he's the other normal one in the family," she said, releasing Cassie.

"Thanks, Michelle. I know he's got a lot more going on than he talked about, which makes this whole move tough, but hey, like he said, we're here for a party and ball game and there's no time for somber moods. Let's go watch the game," she said as she motioned us toward the big-screen television.

Just as Claude Deere predicted, the boys from Georgia put it to the visitors 54-0, and all the partygoers were pleased. Michelle and I excused ourselves shortly after the game was over and left. Later on, we found a nice Italian restaurant nearby and had a relaxed dinner.

On our walk back to the hotel, Michelle took my hand. "Max, I want you to know I'm not the kind of girl who's always running off with some guy for an out-of-town trip," she said. "I'm more likely to stay home and watch old movies or read a book. But to be honest, there's something about you, and it seemed right for me to make this trip. I've had a great time so far today, and when would I ever get a chance to see an incredible mansion like the one we were in? Now I get to walk with a handsome guy down the streets of Atlanta, hand in hand. Yep. It's been a good trip."

We stopped in front of a store closed for the night, and I turned to face her.

"And I can't think of anyone I'd rather be with tonight than you, Michelle," I said. I placed my hands on her waist and we kissed the kind of kiss that takes you to another world. The kind that makes you unaware of time, space, people and things going on around you—a total brain shutdown of everything that's not the kiss. The kind of kiss that says you're with someone special and you don't want the feeling to end.

When we finally separated and my eyes opened, Michelle smiled a huge smile, still with her eyes closed. Perhaps the first look after a kiss tells something, I don't know. But if her smile told how she felt afterwards, I could only return that smile with one like it.

"Oh, Max. How about we go back to our room and have that alone time we've talked about?"

I put my arm around her and we walked at a leisurely pace back to the hotel, still smiling and basking in the glow of the moment.

Chapter Twenty-seven

*T*he next morning I awoke to bright rays of sun coming in through the window. I rolled over to see Michelle still asleep. I became mesmerized as her chest rose gently and fell with each breath, and by her hair that sparkled in the morning sunlight. To stare at someone this long while they were awake would make them feel, well, stared at and uncomfortable. But while she was sleeping, I had a chance to study how pretty she was. My movement and the morning light had no effect on her as she continued regular breathing, sleeping soundly. For a moment, I pondered our evening and this wonderful person who had made the weekend—and really every day since I'd met her— more than enjoyable. She was certainly special to me, and I hoped I was to her.

After showering and getting dressed, I was about to leave the room to get something from the cantina downstairs when Michelle awoke.

"You're not running out on me, are you?" she asked in a sleepy voice.

"No way, sweetheart," I answered. "Just headed downstairs to get some orange juice and something to eat. What can I get for you?"

"How about a nice warm man who'll give me a good morning kiss?" she responded.

"You already have one of those," I answered as I walked over to the bed, brushed back her hair and granted her request.

"That's better," she answered as she placed her head back on the pillow. "My mother always said that the best way to start the day was a kiss from your lover. I assumed she meant my dad, but I never asked her for details." She giggled.

She raised her hand and said, "To answer your question sir, yes. I'd like coffee and one of those sweet rolls with lots of cinnamon and gooey stuff on the top. We can split it."

"Coming right up, lover," I answered as I kissed her again and walked out the door.

After the morning snack and a ride to the airport, we found ourselves boarding the flight home. Since it was early Sunday, not many people were traveling, and we had the row in the plane all to ourselves. Michelle took the window seat and I sat next to her.

After the plane lifted off, I asked Michelle something that I'd been wondering about. I hoped it wouldn't upset her, but I wanted to know.

"Michelle, if you don't mind me asking, what's with the Evan guy? I mean, he doesn't seem like your type."

"Max, sometimes people make mistakes and live to regret it. I regret meeting him. When I first got to Nashville, I really wanted to make friends, so I went to this music showcase. There were some good musicians and singers, and I thoroughly enjoyed their performances. After one of the sets, this really outgoing guy, Evan, came over, introduced himself, and we talked about the artists. He asked me to go to a nearby cafe, and we had a nice visit. I guess I was lonely and he was the only one who'd given me any attention, so I stayed and talked with him. We went out a couple of times with his friends to hear other artists until I began to figure him out."

"And what *did* you figure out?" I asked.

"Turns out that he sort of had a reputation for picking up women at those types of events. Well, when we went out the third time, we heard this new female singer, and he sort of lost interest in me and started hanging around with her. I'd already decided that I didn't want to go out with him again. Shortly afterwards, the girl's music got popular and she got a record deal. She toured with a really big name and left him in her dust. So after he got dumped, he started calling me every now and then, but I never picked up or talked to him. When he showed up in my house the other night, especially in the condition he was in, I was really scared worrying about what he'd do. I'm glad you were there with me," she said in a way that I knew the Evan chapter in her life was over.

"You weren't the only scared one! That guy's a nut case! Unfortunately, there're guys like him all over town—women, too, for that matter—trying to hook up with somebody soon-to-be-famous, hoping they'll roll in the dough with them when they make it. Somehow, I don't think those types of relationships last very long though."

Our plane landed around noon on a beautiful sunny day back home. We got in my car and headed back to Michelle's place. I pulled up the back entrance, then got Michelle's bag out for her.

When we arrived at the door, Michelle said, "Max, I know it's been a long weekend and you're probably ready for a little downtime. I know I am, although it's been wonderful—a weekend I won't soon forget. You will call me tomorrow, won't you?" she asked.

"Of course," I said, giving her a quick kiss on the lips. "And remember we've got a date Tuesday night with Kubrick—for whatever that's about. I guess one more meeting with him won't hurt."

Chapter Twenty-eight

I walked into the office Monday morning and found a manila envelope on the floor, apparently having been slid under the door. It was marked:

Max Jackson; confidential.

I sat at my desk, took out a sword-shaped letter opener and slit the envelope open. Inside was a note and several five-by-seven photos. The note read:

Max,
Don't take me for an idiot. I know what you're doing. Uncle Claude's gonna to kick the bucket soon and some of us cousins reckon

he's got to give away all his millions. Since we're the only living relatives, we figure we get it. At that party in the country, Cassie told me your name. I looked it up and found out you were a private eye! So when I saw you in Atlanta and saw how you knew that lawyer friend of Layla's, who's also her uncle's lawyer, I put one and one together.

I figure that you've done gone and got sold on how sweet Cassie is and that us other cousins are problem children. I bet you've given Cassie a clean report to that lawyer who's helping Uncle Claude. Well I have news for you — the fruit don't fall far from the tree, and Cassie's just like us. Take a gander at these here pictures. You might want to rethink your position. I found them at Cassie's apartment recently and thought they might come in handy someday. Share these with that lawyer buddy of yours so Uncle Claude can see another side of Cassie.

It ain't too late to change your mind. The old man ain't dead yet.

Waiting for justice!

Gabriel F.

I placed the letter on the desk and studied the photos. There were ten five-by-sevens of Cassie in various poses wearing bikini swimsuits in a modeling session of some kind. Her beauty and incredible fitness made her an excellent model. There was nothing lewd about the photos, but I guess getting them to me was Gabriel's way of saying Cassie's not an angel either.

With my door still open while I sat at the desk holding the photos, I heard the now recognizable sound of Michelle's steps as she climbed up the stairs to our floor. She walked around the desk, came up behind me and gave me a hug. She looked over my shoulder and gasped as she saw the photos.

"Those are Cassie's! How did you get them?" she asked.

"They were in an envelope that was slid under my door this morning. According to the note, they're from Gabriel, who got them at Cassie's place. He's figured that I work for Josef Kubrick and that I have some role in what happens to Claude Deere's money when he dies. Ole Gabriel thinks these photos are his ticket to proving that Cassie's no better than him or any other cousins. He may have a point. What do you think, Michelle?"

"Max! I saw these photos the night I was at Cassie's place! She went to her guest bedroom and brought them out for me to see. We'd been talking about our first jobs and she told me that one summer she worked at a community center as a lifeguard and regularly exercised in their gym. One day a woman who was often at the pool gave her a business card. She owned a modeling agency and said they were looking for someone to compete in a fitness model contest that weekend. The short story is that she competed and won first place—one thousand dollars! That was huge money to a teenage lifeguard. My first job didn't pay that much for the whole summer!" she exclaimed.

As I continued to pore over the photos, Michelle said, "I think you've studied them enough, Max." She took the ones I was holding and stuffed them back in the envelope.

"But Michelle, look at what great shape she was in! Check out those abs!" I said.

"That's not all you were looking at, mister! Now concentrate. How *does* this affect your report?"

"Hmmm. I'm getting concerned that whatever Kubrick recommends to Deere is going to piss off somebody and maybe several somebodies," I said. "And it could get messy if Cassie gets all the inheritance or if the symphony and botanical gardens win out. Twenty-million dollars is a whole lot of money."

"Holy cow, Max! I didn't know it was that much!" Michelle exclaimed.

She looked concerned. "I don't want Cassie to get hurt Max, or for her to be put in some kind of bad situation. It's amazing how money complicates things, isn't it? I just want to get back to being plain ole friends with Cassie."

She paused for a minute. "And speaking of changes Max, I've decided that my article on the Tomlin home will be my last in my current line of work. I need to get into something more interesting, away from the world of looking for spirits in scary houses."

"Well, Michelle, you really seem to enjoy writing, but I don't blame you for wanting to shift gears to a more pleasant subject. If you do change careers, you could be a party planner or a PI associate. Heck, from what I've seen, you could do anything!!"

"Thanks, Max, but after being with you, I believe the investigation world is not my cup of tea either. However, I could see myself as an event coordinator and writing promotional documents—that sort of thing," Michelle said confidently.

Michelle had that faraway look in her eyes that said she was serious about making a change. I just hoped she could find another line of work without moving to another city.

She refocused on me. "I better leave you alone to finish your work, and so I can wrap up my story on the Tomlin adventure. As excited about it as I was when I got the offer to do this, it's all I can do to muster the energy to write about our experience that night. The last thing I need is for this article to become really popular and for me to get offers from other folks wanting me to do the same for their place! Wait. I'm thinking out loud too much, Max. Here I am, leaving your office to go to mine. Bye," she said with a wave of her hand as she walked out the door.

Michelle seemed a little despondent over having one job to finish and a new one to discover. I understood it: A state of limbo isn't comfortable for anyone, especially when it's about work. The comfort found in the known entity, even though it may not be the greatest place, sometimes seems preferable to an unknown future. Still, I had a feeling Michelle was determined to make a change for the better and was willing to take a chance.

I placed the envelope in a desk drawer and locked it. The photos needed to get back to Cassie, but I didn't think this was the time to return them.

My phone vibrated and a photo of a policeman's badge appeared. It was Sergeant O'Hara.

"Max here," I answered. "What's up, O'Hara?"

"Nothin' much, Jackson. I was just callin' to remind you about tomorrow night and the guys getting together for my birthday at our watering hole. I also feel like beating someone in darts and naturally thought about you. What da ya say?" He asked with a laugh.

I laughed back.

"You're probably right about my darts skills, but unfortunately, I already have plans for dinner at that very same place tomorrow night. It's sort of a business meeting and date combination. I'll take a rain check," I answered.

"Sure. No worries. I'll be there to celebrate and drown my sorrows, too. I've got to make a couple of arrests tomorrow for a white collar crime that's not going to be pleasant, as if any arrests are. You'll see it in the papers Wednesday. I thought being with friends and some beer would lighten the evening. Maybe I'll see you there and meet your date!'

"Yeah. You'd like Michelle. Sorry to let you down, O'Hara, but the business meeting is with that lawyer from Atlanta, so I really can't change it. Let's shoot for another time," I said.

"Oh! And happy birthday O'Hara!" I added.

"Roger that, Jackson," the sergeant said as he hung up.

Chapter Twenty-nine

*T*uesday morning, I received a text from Josef Kubrick stating that his plane would arrive at five-thirty and that he and Layla would meet us at seven for dinner. I sent him the address of the restaurant after thinking twice about offering to pick him up at the airport. I wanted to be hospitable, but I didn't think riding with him and Layla from the airport and back would be a good idea.

Before it got too hot, I went outside to wash the car for my big date. It hadn't been cleaned in weeks and certainly looked like it.

"You missed that chrome piece underneath the door, Mr. Clean!" It was Colonel Canyon, standing on his front porch.

"Stand back a few feet and bend down so you can see it," he instructed. "You want to make a good impression on her, don't you? Be sure and wipe down the painted part just inside the door, too! They always see that."

"What makes you think I'm tryin' to impress a girl, Colonel?" I called out to him from the driveway.

"I can read you like a book, Jackson, just like my wet-behind-the-ears recruits in the Army. You've had a silly grin on your face ever since you stepped outside, and you've been whistling the same dang tune over and over to boot. 'Bout to drive me crazy! I figure it's that girl that's got you so worked up. What's up with you two, anyway?"

"Something, I think. But now she's talking about changing jobs and I'm concerned that she might move away," I said, thinking that it probably wouldn't happen but could, and man, that would be a major bummer.

"What? And leave a catch like you? Can't say that I blame her!" he said with a laugh.

"Just kiddin' lover boy, but mind my word," he continued. "Somebody cute and feisty won't last long in this town. Your competition might scoop her up if you don't scoop first. I'd say you better make sure she knows how you feel about her or it's curtains for you!"

"You're really on a roll today, Colonel! First I get a car-cleaning critique and now lessons on love. Not everyone has such a helpful neighbor," I said.

"Just doin' my job, son. Doin' my job. By the way, I'm headed to Andy Jack's for dinner tonight. Maybe some cute thing will take a shine to an old fella like me," he said with a grin.

"That's where I'm taking Michelle tonight! We're meeting a guy from Atlanta with his date. It's sort of a business meeting dinner date. Maybe you can meet her if you don't go too early for the early bird Senior special!" I said, smiling.

"Ha! Got me there, son. That's a good one! See you later."

The Colonel went back inside his house groaning and bent over like a really old man, laughing as he braced his hand on his back and pretended to limp.

I finally finished with the car and remembered that I hadn't talked to Michelle today. She certainly needed our dinner plans before it got close to time to go. So, I gave her a call.

Ring. Ring. Ring. No answer, but I left a message.

"Hey, Michelle! Max here. Dinner tonight is at seven with Kubrick and Layla. They'll meet us at the restaurant. I'll pick you up at

6:45. Casual dress. My neighbor Colonel Canyon and police Sergeant O'Hara said they'd be there, too, although they're not part of our group. Call me if you need anything! Ah, love you."

I hung up and thought about my last words that just sort of popped out. *Love you.* I guess I could have said *I love you,* but somehow all three words sounded more serious than just *love you.* Did my real feelings for her somehow come out in a spur-of-the-moment statement at the end of the message? All I wanted to do was inform her about dinner, then *bam,* I end the message with *love you.*

Since Michelle only lived about five minutes away, I planned to leave at 6:35 in order to be on time. I'd noticed that she was always prompt and even early for things we'd done together, so I decided to not mess with her expectations about timeliness.

I closed the back door on the way out and put the car in reverse down the driveway, only to find a familiar truck blocking my exit to the street. When I got out to investigate, I heard a truck door close and saw Gabriel get out.

"So, Mr. PI man. You check out them pictures?" he said with a nasty grin. He leaned back against the truck and crossed his arms.

"Sure did, Gabriel. Do you want them back?" I answered, ignoring the intent of his question.

He straightened up and said, "I don't want 'em back, but I wanna make sure a certain uncle of mine in Atlanta sees them or bad things might happen."

Behind me and to my left I heard a familiar screech as Colonel Canyon's screen door opened. Gabriel and I both turned to see him carrying his rifle and cleaning supplies in hand. He sat down and spoke to us.

"Don't mind me at all boys. I'm just gonna clean out ole Betsy here. Never know when she might come in handy." He stood with only the rifle in hand and asked, "By the way, is everything okay out there?"

"We're okay, Colonel. This guy was just moving his truck so I could get out of my driveway. Weren't you?" I said looking dead-eye to Gabriel.

"Sure. I'm outta here, but don't say I didn't warn you!" Gabriel replied with a finger pointed in my direction.

He climbed back in the truck and started up the diesel with a pedal-to-the-floor rev that caused a big cloud of black smoke to billow from the exhaust pipe. The agitated driver and truck roared off down the street at a brisk pace to who knows where.

"Thanks, neighbor," I called out to Colonel Canyon.

"Don't mention it. That PI business must be tougher than I thought. Now get on before you're late for your date!" he answered back.

Michelle ran out her front door to meet me as I arrived at her house.

"Anxious to see me?" I asked, as she opened the door and hoped in the passenger seat.

"Always," she answered. "You're always on time if you're not early, so I decided to just look out the front window and come out when you arrived. This meeting seemed important and I didn't want to make you late."

"Frankly, I'm not sure what's up. I just know Kubrick wanted to meet me tonight. I figure it's about the Deere case, but who knows? What's interesting is that Cassie's cousin Layla is with him. That makes me think it's more of a personal thing—a thank you for the information I got for him."

Andy Jack's Brewery was comfortable in the way an old shoe is—broken in just right after years of wear. Friendly and lively patrons made for a cheerful setting, and the walls were decorated with autographed photos of musicians, celebrities and politicians who'd frequented the restaurant. Oak wood floors and original tin ceiling tiles dated the place, which had survived a couple of small fires and only one change in ownership over the years. It was truly an icon of restaurant history in this part of town.

I waved to the assistant manager, my friend Michael, who motioned us over to a table in a back corner. It was about as private as any in the small restaurant and had the benefit of a window overlooking the parking lot.

After we'd been seated a few minutes, I told Michelle, "It looks like our guests have arrived." A car with an Uber sign in the corner of the windshield pulled in at the side entrance carrying Kubrick and Layla.

When they entered the restaurant, I stood up and motioned for them to join us. We said hellos, shook hands, then sat down. The two were quite a contrast as they pored over the menu: Kubrick, carrying a small leather folio, was stocky but distinguished looking, with salt and pepper hair and a pale complexion. He was way over-dressed for this place. And then there was Layla, a petite, deeply tanned, bleach-blonde in a yellow sundress, carrying a large purse and smacking a piece of gum. She was clearly self-absorbed, with a persona that suggested a free spirit and maybe a loose cannon, too.

I also couldn't help but think that since Kubrick was dating Layla, this was *his* way to weasel into his friend's fortune and get a pretty young woman in the process. He had to know that I'd figured that out! Originally, he just mentioned Layla as a step-niece and didn't give any other information. So, was my work just a cover for him to do as he wished?

After we ordered, we talked about their flight into town, how the restaurant smelled like a mix between home-cooked hamburgers and fajitas, and the football party where her Uncle Claude informed everyone about his move. The conversation seemed a little forced to me, but that's about all we had in common.

With not much else to say in the otherwise noisy restaurant, Michelle broke our silence with, "So, are you two a couple or what? How did you meet?"

Leave it to assistant PI McCartney to get things started again and press for information.

Layla smiled, and reached for Kubrick's hand. "We met quite by accident one day this past spring. You see, I was visiting a girlfriend—her name's Marcia—down in Atlanta, and thought it would be nice to check in on my dear old uncle. I called and he said we could come over to visit and could use the pool if we wanted to. Well, it was hot for a day in April, and wading in a pool sounded wonderful. Especially at his place! Did you see that pool? Anyway, Marcia and I were working on our tans when guess who showed up?"

She leaned over to Kubrick, gave him a peck on the cheek and giggled.

"Josef was at the house on business with my uncle, but before he left, he gave me his business card, and told me he was looking for some temporary executive assistant help since one of his was out with a broken arm. Well, I started the job the next Monday, he liked my work, and just like that, we started dating. Isn't that exciting?! The temp job will be over soon, and I guess then we'll let everyone know about our relationship." She paused and looked him straight in the eyes as she batted her own. "In all his years, poor Josef never found that special someone. Till now."

Oh, brother, I thought. *Give me a break.* Her sappiness was giving me heartburn.

"Congratulations, you two! You do look like a happy couple!" said Michelle.

Yeah. A single eligible lawyer and a foxy gold-digger surfer girl separated in age by two decades. A match made in heaven.

Our one-sided conversation continued during dinner. Layla bragged about how close she was to her uncle. Then she talked about clients she'd conversed with at her bartending job in Florida, and how because of this great experience, she'd considered going back to school to get a degree in psychology to become a counselor. Fortunately dinner arrived quickly and we got to eat in relative peace.

After a while, Kubrick broke the silence.

"Well, besides being the cutest woman on my side of town, Layla has some great office skills," Kubrick said. "She single-handedly cleaned up our office files, edited some work for me, and even put together your report. That's actually the reason for my visit."

Kubrick unzipped the folio, pulled out a few papers and handed them to me.

"Here you go, Jackson. I need you to sign this one for my records and the other one is a copy for you."

The documents were printed on official Kubrick, Goldmeister and Klein letterhead and at first glance looked okay. But before I signed next to my typed name on the second page, I read the summary paragraph to make sure it was correct. It read:

So from my perspective, I would advise your client that Cassie Simpshire is a good person, but that evidence against other cousins does not appear to be enough to keep them from receiving inheritance, as well. As a matter of fact, certain new information convinces me to think you should direct the inheritance to Layla Farasinni, as I hear she is the only one to visit her uncle prior to the party in Atlanta and seems to genuinely care about him. Honoring the bassoons in the orchestra or roses at the botanical gardens would be nice, but if it were me, I'd pass it on to a real live human being in my family — a loving, caring person like Layla.

"I can't sign this, Josef! Someone changed my last paragraph, changing my recommendation from Cassie to Layla!" I stood up from my chair and tossed the papers back to him.

"I wonder how that could have happened," Layla said coyly. "And to think, Uncle Claude has already seen this report and will soon be instructing his trusted friend to write it in the will. It wouldn't be wise for dear Josef to say that the first report he received wasn't correct. That would make him look like a fool. And that wouldn't be good, would it darling?"

"I, ah, don't know what to say, Jackson. I mean, she's got a point. I'll try to make amends with Claude Deere, but sometimes when he gets an idea in his head, it's hard to change it," he said apologetically. "I never intended for something like this to happen."

"I don't know who to believe," I said. "But it looks like the two of you are conspiring to get the money for yourselves. And you Kubrick, letting Layla take the blame! I'm making a call to Atlanta as soon as I get home and explain the whole thing to him."

I extended my hand for Michelle to get up.

"We're leaving! Why don't you take care of the bill?" I said glaring at Layla.

She reached for Kubrick's wallet in his outside jacket pocket, pulled out a one hundred dollar bill and slammed it on the table.

"That ought to take care of it!" she said spitefully.

All four of us left the table and hurriedly walked toward the entrance in the now-crowded business. People were everywhere. All the tables were full, all stools at the bar were taken and several patrons were standing around the entrance waiting for others to leave. One guy, who was in even a bigger hurry than we were, pushed through the crowd, stopped our progress, and knocked Michelle to the floor in the process. He didn't even turn to help her up or acknowledge that he'd done anything. Just kept on walking.

I reached down to help the stunned Michelle get up and to make sure she was okay.

"Hold your horses, pal!" yelled out an older gentleman with a familiar voice who stepped right in front of the guy in a hurry. "Watch where you're goin!"

The familiar voice was the Colonel, who evidently made it for dinner and not with the early birds.

"Outta' my way, old man!" the guy said as he swept his arm out to move the Colonel from his path. But Canyon ducked and the assailant's arm missed his target. The Colonel responded with a right upper-cut that landed squarely under the guy's chin, a haymaker that knocked him down and out for several moments.

Another familiar face came running over, shouting, "Police, Police! Break it up!"

Sergeant O'Hara had witnessed the scene from the bar and started the process of pulling both Colonel Canyon and his groggy would-be assailant to the door and outside to settle them down. After several minutes of talking to the two men, he let them go. The Colonel returned inside to a cheering crowd and the other guy went to his car still holding his chin and shaking his head.

Michelle and I walked outside, as did Layla and Kubrick. They followed us to my car parked in the narrow secluded alley behind the restaurant.

"I'm sorry about the report, Max. I'll do what I can to make things right," Kubrick said as we stopped at the car.

Layla separated herself from us by about six feet, moving away from the car with her back to the restaurant. She reached into her purse and pulled out a Smith and Wesson .38 revolver.

"No, you won't!" Layla said. A sinister look replaced the put-on smile she usually wore.

"What do you think you're doing?" yelled Kubrick, flabbergasted.

"I'm making sure you don't do anything stupid and mess up my future," she said. "The three of you know too much and are going to have to be eliminated."

"Hold on, Layla," I said. "If we're found dead, you'll be the primary suspect. A hundred people could have seen us in the restaurant and the guy at the door when we left was a policeman. You'll be arrested, found guilty, and will spend the rest of your life in jail, if you're not executed. Now, put down the gun."

Michelle pleaded. "I can sort of understand you wanting to kill Max and maybe me, but why would you kill Josef, your sweetheart?"

Layla looked at him. "Sweetheart, maybe, and he's no doubt very influential as far as my uncle goes. Why do you think I took the job working for him? I thought I'd get close to the action with my uncle, but never dreamed I'd have access to the very papers that could determine my future! He played right into my hands. But that's all behind us now."

In the distance behind Layla, I saw Gabriel's big truck pull into a parking spot as he looked in our direction. He placed his arm outside the open driver's window and to watch the action from afar.

"So I see you've arranged for your getaway," I said, nodding toward Gabriel's truck.

Layla took her eyes off us and twisted around slightly to see Gabriel in the distance who waved to her. While she was turned toward him, distracted, I leaned forward and sprung at her. I grabbed her wrist with one hand and the barrel of the gun with the other. With one snap of the wrist, it fell from her hand and I got her in a hammerlock. She fought and kicked to get away, but to no avail. Kubrick kicked the gun to where she couldn't reach it, then helped me pin her against my car.

"I'll go get your policeman friend!" Michelle yelled, racing toward the restaurant entrance.

"Let me go! Let me go!" Layla cried, still bucking and kicking to get free.

I looked toward Gabriel's truck, thinking reinforcements for Layla would be on the way. But then I saw the driver's window go up, and the truck quickly pulled out of its parking space and headed toward 21st.

Moments later Michelle and Sergeant O'Hara came running around the corner and toward us.

"What's goin' on here, Jackson? Michelle said something about a woman pullin' a gun on you!"

Layla had finished her wrestling match and calmed down. She stood between Kubrick and me, despondent and crying.

"She's the one, O'Hara," I answered.

"All that money," Layla sobbed. "My plan was working till I looked around for Gabriel. By the way, where is that no-good..." she said looking where his truck had been parked.

"He took off as soon as the gun fell out of your hand," I said. "I guess he didn't want to get caught up in your idiotic plan. Sergeant, you might want to put out an APB for a black, late-model F-150 Raptor diesel with a bumper sticker about Smith and Wesson driven by a Gabriel Farasinni. He was about to be her get-away driver."

"Will do. And I've called for back-up," O'Hara said. "They should be here any minute. Now tell me what happened, Jackson."

I replayed the details of our meeting to the sergeant, the events during dinner and what happened when we went outside. I explained how I distracted Layla to get the gun, and how we held her down till he arrived.

"And where's the gun?" he asked.

"Right over there," I said, as I pointed to where it rested in front of a nearby car's back tire.

"Okay, y'all stay here and leave everything where it is," O'Hara said as a police car pulled up.

The officers hustled over to us and Sergeant O'Hara briefly explained what happened. One officer took a couple of photos of the gun on the ground before he picked it up with a gloved hand and placed it in a plastic bag. Then he took a couple photos of the crime scene. After a brief discussion, they read Layla her rights, handcuffed her, and escorted her to the back of the cruiser.

"That was close!" said Kubrick. "I never dreamed she'd do something that crazy. I mean, pulling a gun on the three of us and thinking she'd get away with it? The things some people will do for money never cease to amaze me."

"Me either," I said as I glared right at Kubrick.

"You were more than brave, Max," Michelle said. "Thanks for saving us."

"Yeah! Thanks,," echoed Kubrick.

"Don't mention it. You know, I'm not sure Layla thought this out very well. Obviously, Gabriel was in it and was going to pick her up after she got rid of us. I noticed she was nervous, didn't hold the gun very steady. I'm not sure she really would have shot us. The whole thing doesn't make sense."

Kubrick took a deep breath and exhaled it slowly. "If you folks will excuse me, I've got a flight to Atlanta to catch and a long heart-to-heart to schedule with an old friend about how our firm handled his job," he said. "I think he'll understand, knowing the cast of characters, and they really are... There's my Uber, right on time."

"Great. Safe travels, Kubrick."

"Will do, Jackson," he said. "And nice to see you again, Michelle. Sorry I got you into this mess."

"That's okay, Josef. Everything turned out okay," replied Michelle, who had settled down and now looked relieved.

Sergeant O'Hara approached us. "Well folks, since y'all were part of a barroom fight and then held at gunpoint by that woman, I'd say that you've had enough excitement on what was supposed to be my birthday celebration. Why don't you go home where it's safe, and I'll go back inside the restaurant and finish my dinner that never got started?"

"Good plan, O'Hara. For all of us! I'm glad you were around tonight and I appreciate you taking care of business," I said.

"That's what I'm here for, Jackson."

Chapter Thirty

The next morning I went to the gym, had a good workout and shower, then made my way to work. I stopped at the Happy Bean and Bagel, but found a sign on the door that said they were closed because of a death in the family. Many of the folks who worked there were related, so I understood their reason for closing, but still I hadn't had breakfast. I was really looking forward to one of those cinnamon rolls!

I remembered a new place down the street that advertised delivery and gave them a call. I ordered, and they assured me my breakfast would be there in thirty minutes. My growling stomach certainly hoped so.

The Jackson Private Investigations mailbox downstairs was empty except for a small spider that scurried away when I opened the door. There weren't even any advertisements.

My trip upstairs was quiet, which was odd for a Wednesday morning. No light was coming from Michelle's office and the entry door for the shrink's office still had a "closed" sign hanging outside. All the silence felt a bit eerie, even for me.

I entered my office and turned on the lights and an oscillating fan that I knew would get the air circulating. The place was stuffy and needed some fresh air.

Then I took a seat and fired up my computer. A quick login to my office mail didn't show any leads or requests for my services. I checked *The Tennessean* online to see what was going on and found an incredibly dull day about town. I guess they hadn't heard about our altercations in South Nashville, but then, that was only big news to us.

For the first time in a long while, I officially thought things were looking kind of bleak in my investigations business. I did need to deposit that check from Kubrick and send him my expenses from travel last weekend, but that was about all I had to do. I was caught up. There had been a lot of excitement the last few days, so I guess I was coming off a high from all that activity. Now I was getting a little nervous about my next job.

A ringing phone interrupted my blues. It was Josef Kubrick, of all people, hopefully about to give me some good news and get me out of the current funk I was in.

"Hello, Josef. You're at it early this morning," I said.

"Mornin' Max. I want to apologize about yesterday and not telling you about Layla and me. And since then, I realized I had a lot of things to correct down here in Atlanta. I had to apologize to my office staff for hiring that looney-tunes girl Layla and fix any other damage that she did to the place. But most importantly, I visited with my friend Claude Deere an hour ago and set the record straight with him about Layla, your investigation, and his original charge to me. I think we got things worked out. He's decided to follow his gut feeling and do what *we've* recommended: that Cassie be the heir to his estate. I drew up the papers and he signed them this morning."

"That's great, Josef. It sounds like you got everything straightened out. I'm glad he made that decision."

Kubrick continued. "Claude said he doesn't have much longer to live—maybe a couple of months. He doesn't look too bad, and even though he's in a lot of pain, he refuses to take the strong pain pills. The doctor told him it will hit him hard here in the next couple of months. Damn, it's hard to see that awful disease take someone's life. Especially a close friend and client like Claude."

"I can't agree with you more, Josef." I paused.

"I told you that Cassie heard about her uncle's illness and word got out from there," I said. "I think maybe Layla found out from Gabriel who heard it from Cassie, who was told about it by her boyfriend who worked in the lab in Atlanta. That explains why Layla was so interested in visiting her uncle recently and one reason why she was interested in you, not that you don't have other redeeming qualities, I'm sure. Getting closer to her uncle and working for and dating his lawyer put her in a great position to manipulate things in her favor, even though her half-baked plan didn't work."

"Yes, sadly, it all makes sense and I fell for it," he said. "Well, I'd better get back to my work. I've got a lot to catch up on from yesterday. Thanks for your help in all this, Max. Keep in touch."

"Will do, Josef," I answered.

Several minutes later I heard three gentle raps on the door.

"Hi, Max," Michelle called out as she peeked her head inside.

"Would you come over to my office for a minute?" she asked. "That is, if you're not too busy."

"Sure," I answered, as I stood up to join her. "I'm about as un-busy as a person could get."

When I walked into her office, I noticed several stacks of boxes in a corner next to the door, and that all her pictures had been taken off the wall.

"What's up, Michelle? It looks like you're moving out."

Michelle looked up at me, placed a book she was holding into a box and said gently, "Please sit down, Max."

Chapter Thirty-one

My original concern with Michelle's interest in the case with Cassie was that she would get too involved and it would eventually wear on her. In the process, she'd have an opportunity to get to know the real me ... and might not be very impressed. I surmised that she'd figured it was time to fish or cut bait, and cutting bait won out.

I took a place on the love seat as she pulled up the desk chair instead of sitting with me. Michelle's demeanor that told me what she was about to say was important and she wanted my complete attention.

"Max, yesterday was quite a day. I mean, we met some people we hardly knew for dinner, witnessed a neighbor of yours punch out a guy for knocking me down, had a gun pulled on us and nearly got shot. And then there's all the anguish about my friend Cassie, her family, and I don't know what all else. And that was just the last week or so!!" she said.

So far, this wasn't going well. Michelle moved from the desk chair to the love seat with me and placed my right hand between her hands which rested partially on her knees and some on mine. She looked down at the floor briefly, took a deep breath and looked me in the eye.

"Max, these last couple of weeks since I've gotten to know you have been some of the most fun and exciting days of my life. I've enjoyed your sense of humor, your ability to make decisions and to get things done, not to mention the fact that you were very brave and saved my life yesterday. That was awesome, and I thank you."

She took another deep breath, looked at our hands, squeezed them, then looked back at me.

"So?" I said ready for the dagger to strike.

"So, since I've decided that my article on the Tomlin home would be the last for me in the ghosts and apparitions world, I'm going to move my office into my house and dedicate myself full time to writing a novel, like I've been wanting to do and maybe something else. I'll save money on office rent and eating out so much," she said.

"That explains the boxes and pictures off the wall," I answered assuming she was done.

"There's more, Max."

Oh, great! There's more, I thought.

"Max, I don't know what you'll think about me when I say this, but well, I couldn't sleep last night thinking about it. You see, I've never met anyone like you. You have an assortment of qualities that I never thought I'd admire in a man, but I do! Sometimes you drive me absolutely crazy. But deep down in my heart, I think you're special to me and I hope I am to you, too," she said sincerely, with that special kindness unique to her.

I enjoyed this part of Michelle's outpouring much better than how she started, but was still tense waiting for the inevitable knockout punch. She took another deep breath and zeroed in on my eyes.

"Max, would you consider moving in with me? You know, sharing my house with me?" Michelle asked in a tone as serious as a judge announcing a guilty verdict. "My place is paid for, and you could sell yours and not have a mortgage. I could clean out that small bedroom on the second floor and you could use it as an office. And I could make cinnamon rolls and coffee in the morning to make it smell like this old office space. We'd get to see each other a lot more then. And then maybe, maybe I wouldn't lose you and you wouldn't lose me." She let out a long breath. "There, I said it."

Michelle looked with expectant eyes at me.

"Wow, Michelle! That's quite a proposition. Let me get this straight. You decided all this last night?" I asked the first question on my mind, half in disbelief and half in wonder.

"No, I started to fall in love with you the night you took me home from the ER, when I was drowsy and falling asleep. You gently placed a blanket on me and kissed me right here," she said, pointing to her forehead. "There was just something about that little act of kindness that started me thinking seriously about you, and I have been ever since. I hope I'm not being too forward, Max, but I want you to know how I feel. So there. If you think I'm crazy, just tell me and I'll go," she said, obviously looking for my answer.

I reached for Michelle's hands and held them as we both stood up.

"I think it sounds like a wonderful idea, and I'm really excited that you asked." I hugged her with all my might.

"No, I don't think you're crazy—not too crazy anyway—and I really appreciate you telling me how you feel. Sometimes I hold my feelings inside and don't say or do the things I should. So when do we start?" I asked.

Michelle responded with one of those tight hugs that said she didn't want to let me go. I felt tear drops fall from her cheeks to mine as she held on.

"How about today?" she answered as she sniffed and wiped back another tear. "We can fill up my car then put some things in yours."

"Sure. It's a good thing we've got my car, too. If we just had your Miata, we'd have to make a million trips!" I said.

"That's my Max," she said. "Always with the jokes! Here. Let's take a couple of boxes downstairs on the first trip."

"Would you be up for celebrating tonight, Michelle?" I asked.

"Sure! Where would you like to go?" Michelle answered leaning back still with her arms around my waist.

"I know a romantic place in the Gulch with white tablecloths, candles on the tables, and a pianist who plays soft music as long as you toss a tip in the glass," I told her.

"Ooh, let's go there. I'll wear my little black dress with the sequined spaghetti straps," Michelle said dreamily.

"I can't wait to see that! And I'll wear my navy coat and khaki pants like I do anytime I go somewhere fancy." I laughed. "Maybe after dessert we drop by Beauregard's and check out his collection of lonely diamond rings."

Michelle's eyes lit up and we hugged tightly again.

"I'd like that very much, Max."

We finally broke our hug and each picked up a box to take to our cars. I figured I'd have to start packing my own office soon, but that could wait for another day.

As we walked out of Michelle's office toward the stairwell and got to my office door, I noticed it was held ajar by a medium-sized cardboard package. Michelle set her box down and leaned over to check it out.

"Look, Max. There's a note on top of the box. It says '*Max Jackson, PI. Fragile! Personal and confidential!!*'"

The End

Epilogue

As time passed, Michelle and I adjusted to our new living arrangement. I became quite successful, if you count working all the time as successful, doing private investigations for a number of clients. Michelle's new work in event-planning and marketing kept her busy at home and in town. Her agent had pitched her novel to several publishing companies. We're still waiting to hear back. Michelle occasionally helped with my investigations as she did in Cassie's case.

Sergeant O'Hara and his staff worked with the Atlanta police to find the guy who delivered the package, but so far had no leads. They also continued to try to locate the family of the driver who was shot. Charges were pending against his assailant.

Police also managed to find a witness who, prior to the fire at Cassie's store, saw a man wearing a hoodie throw something in the back window of the place, but there was no positive ID and the arsonist was never found. Damage to Winner's Threads wasn't excessive, and Cassie was able to reopen in two months to a large crowd of loyal customers.

After Josef Kubrick worked things out with Claude Deere, he settled back into his law practice and even referred a *couple of cases to me over the next year. They were different from the first one and Kubrick didn't get involved.*

Layla Farasinni was charged with three counts of aggravated assault, as well as fraud charges related to altered documents at the legal office and would likely be in jail for a long time. She was a nut-case in my book and I was glad to see justice served.

My pal Colonel Canyon got his picture on the wall at Andy Jack's for his boxing skills. We missed seeing each other after I moved to Michele's place, but he joined us for supper every now and then.

Gabriel Farasinni was questioned regarding the incident at the restaurant, but since there was no incriminating evidence, he wasn't charged. Gabriel was last seen working as a maintenance man at a Las Vegas casino.

The Tomlins sold their home to a young couple who planned to start an organic vegetable farm and rent out extra rooms as an Airbnb.

Claude Deere surprised his doctors by responding well to a new treatment, giving hopes for a little more time in his new home.

Made in the USA
Coppell, TX
11 May 2021